MW00779788

Death by Naked Ladies

A Clean Cozy Mystery with a Bit of Ooh-la-la

Christa Bakker

Counting Blessings

Contents

1

Can I stay here?

The Harley stopped on my driveway just as I stepped outside to get my breakfast baguette. The loose leather jacket and closed helmet told me nothing about my daybreak visitor, drawing my eyes to the faded jeans stretched over his muscles. That was some pair of legs getting off that machine. He turned towards the house and lifted the helmet, freeing floppy gold locks that shimmered in the early morning sunlight.

My breath caught in my throat when I recognised him.

'Thibault?'

He flashed me a smile that could dazzle the neighbours across the valley.

Oh. My. Lady. The nerdy seventeen-year-old had grown up since I last saw him. 'You look good.'

'Thanks. I wish I could say the same.'

Oh, it was him all right. My ex's nephew, the spotted one in a family of black sheep. At least parts of him were decent. Though his name was Thibault, everyone called him Beau.

It used to be sort of a teasing nickname, but apparently he'd grown into it.

'What happened?' I asked, gesturing up and down his body.

He grinned. 'I figured out that life gets easier if you look like you can handle it.'

Did he now? 'So what brings you here?'

He raked a hand through his hair and unzipped his jacket, trying to hide a flash of embarrassment. Then the dimples were back in place. 'I escaped.'

Uh-oh. How old was he now? About ten years my junior, if I remembered correctly... Twenty-one. Hm. 'So?'

'So can I stay here?'

Like I didn't see that one coming. He was a nice guy, but I wasn't keen on renewing contact with my ex-in-laws. My hesitation broke his cool.

'Look, Julie, I wouldn't have come here if I had anywhere else to go. You're the most normal person I know, even though you take pictures of people's butts. Please?'

'My *photographs* are vintage-style pin-ups. I call them art.' The glint of sunlight on chrome caught my eye as I chewed the inside of my lip. 'Is that a '59 Harley-Davidson Duo-Glide?'

His face went suspicious. 'Yyyeeeeees?'

'If you let me use it in a shoot, you can stay the night.'

'Two.'

I scrunched my eyes at him.

He held his palms up. 'Come on, that's my baby! And you've got to give me a fighting chance. Maybe I can help you out with something?'

I eyed him again, still not sure what to make of this. 'Are those working muscles or gym muscles?'

With a mischievous smirk he grabbed me by the waist and lifted me above his head.

'All right! All right, you can stay. Put me down!' When I was back on my feet, I straightened my pencil skirt. 'Idiot,' I muttered. Still, he was a charming idiot. I wondered if he'd let me photograph him.

He shrugged and turned to pick up his backpack. On the back of his leather jacket was an embroidered emblem of the Beaujolais Bikers with his name, spelled T-Bo, across the top. A biker in my house. This was such a bad idea. Oblivious to my thoughts, Beau turned the lion's head doorknob in the middle of the white wooden door and ambled into my personal – private – space. 'Where do I sleep?'

I hurried after him and blocked his path before he could get past the kitchen. I did not want him getting comfortable here. 'There's a spare bedroom above my studio. I use it as a changing room if I have a group shoot. You' – I waved my index finger at him, imitating the way I'd seen his mother do it – 'are to vacate the room, if not the premises, when there are naked women around!'

He uttered a dramatic sigh, but then nodded. 'Okay. Where is it?'

I marched him back outside and led the way along the high wall connecting the house with the large barn that now functioned as my studio. In the middle of that wall, a couple of huge wooden doors led to the courtyard created by the house's L-shape. We could have gone through the kitchen and crossed the courtyard to my studio from there, but I wanted it to be quite clear that he was not to invade my life any more than absolutely necessary.

The main house retained its 1770s façade, but other than an enormous yellow stone fireplace and some cupboards built into the wall, nothing of the old farmhouse remained. Most of the houses in this part of the Beaujolais had enormous cellars with wine presses and tanks, but mine had been a farm all those centuries, not a winery. It did leave me with a big barn, though, and for my purposes, that was much more practical.

A new glass front door was the first thing I'd put in after my great-aunt had signed the property over to me. I had used all my savings to turn the barn into the glorious modern studio we were now entering, but that door was the crowning glory. Every time I opened it, it was as though I was opening the door to my new life. My studio had been finished only three months ago, but because it was made to my specific design, it felt as though it had always been a part of me. It just needed that door so I could open it up.

Most of the walls inside were white, to make the most of the light, but colourful forties and fifties memorabilia and props in strategic places added life to the space. The life of a Golden Age Hollywood movie star.

I still can't believe how lucky I am to be doing this. Plenty of women love to be photographed as a fifties pin-up. Not the feathers-and-corsets kind, mind you. The whoops-did-my-skirt-just-fly-up kind. It's not the shape or the size of the woman, it's the sass. Every woman has that sass, and I love to draw it out and capture it with my camera.

As he entered my studio, Beau pointed out the collection of beautiful bottoms on the wall, both bountiful and more economically sized. 'I like the variety.'

I shrugged. 'I don't like to discriminate. Everyone has a right to look pretty.'

'As long as they pay you for it, huh?'

'Girl's gotta live. Do you want to stay here or not?'

He hurried along, passing my office on the left and the little kitchen area on the right, behind which an open spiral staircase led to the bedroom. Upstairs had the same white walls as my studio below, but in contrast to the polished concrete downstairs, the dark stained wooden floorboards lent this space a homey feel. Instead of buying more streamlined furniture, I'd decorated with some of the classic pieces my aunt had left behind. Most of my clients never saw this floor anyway. I only used it for larger groups so they could change together instead of having to cram into the small dressing area downstairs.

Thibault gave the place a short, appraising look and threw his backpack into a corner.

I folded my arms. 'Will it do, your majesty?'

'I'll be gracious about it.'

I huffed. 'Right. Bathroom through here...'

'Oh good, plenty of room for all my creams and tonics.'

I glared at his tiny backpack but decided to let it pass. 'Kitchen over here.'

'That's not a kitchen. The bathroom is bigger!'

'You'll only be here for two nights. Leave the gourmet meals until you find another kitchen to sleep in.' I was beginning to wonder why I'd let him stay in the first place. Old time's sake, I supposed.

He only grumbled a little at that, probably realising his situation did not allow him to antagonise me. An odd mix of sweet and sour emotions rolled over his face. 'Thank you, Juju.'

I bit my lip, knowing full well why I'd let him in. He was a happy little puppy in a home full of mean old junkyard dogs. I could never have turned him away. But if his happy little puppy dog eyes got to me, he might not see the necessity of leaving my man-free sanctuary sooner rather than later.

'Don't mention it.' I turned towards the stairs. 'I was actually on my way to the *boulangerie*. Do you want something?'

'I ate, thanks.'

As I descended the spiral stairs, he threw himself outstretched onto the sofa opposite the bed, rubbing his face with his hands. Escaped, huh? I was dying to know what that meant, but now clearly wasn't the right time to ask. I always thought he was quite happy living with his mother, but then, I hadn't talked to him in five years. He'd tell me what had happened in due time. Maybe nothing, maybe everything, but it was probably best that he'd left. Even with Franck out of the picture, that family was nothing but a bad influence. And they didn't deal too well with curiosity...

Fancy coming here, though! He must really have had nowhere else to go. We hadn't seen each other since before my divorce. I shuddered. Best to leave the past in the past for now. I'd have to revisit it soon enough if Beau would open up.

My stomach rumbled as I closed the door to the studio behind me. I'm not usually an early riser, but after waking at six I hadn't been able to fall back asleep. I'd decided to get an early start on my paperwork. Since the bakery didn't open until seven, I'd had to postpone breakfast. Even more with the unexpected arrival of Blondie. But he was now safely tucked away, and I was determined to continue with my regular day.

Golden-red vines rustling around me, I drank in the crisp morning air. Autumn really is the best time to be in the Beaujolais. I said hello to a *gendarme* crawling up a wall, but since that's what we call a certain red and black beetle, he took no notice. Pulling my cardigan closer around me, I stepped on my still long shadow. Leaving this little village nine years ago had felt like a liberation, but returning to it after all that had happened was a true homecoming. The familiar smiles, the lack of noise apart from insects and bird song, the explosion of sweetness from a dark purple grape stolen off the vine – it all filled me with a warm sense of belonging.

Saint-Maurice was still the same. I don't think I was. Thibault's arrival had got me remembering my time in Villefranche. I had only been there for eight years. Eight looong years. No, that wasn't fair. I'd loved it at first. When Franck was still fun. But he'd messed with my head and my life enough that it took me a long time, even after I'd got back in touch with people from my old life, to accept my great-aunt's offer and return to Saint-Maurice. I'd lived in limbo for months while they were working on my studio, coming over in every free hour from Villefranche, a ten-minute drive away. With the completion of my beloved studio, I'd gladly said farewell to Villefranche to return to a village where I both did and did not belong. But this? This countryside, this view? Oh, they were more than part of me. They were all of me.

My aunt's – *my* – house was located just outside the village, on a gorgeous plot of land on the sunny side of a valley, surrounded by vineyards. This past summer, I had my clients take their pictures in or beside the little stream that ran across the valley. With the foliage overhead, it was often cooler than the pool I'd secretly put in behind the house. I was still waiting for my brother to blab about that to my aunt. She'd never expressly forbidden its construction, but we all knew she saw pools as new-money status symbols. She – and other relatives – had already said plenty about what I do for a living and how it might soil the family name. Strangely, the mumblings had died down somewhat now that my weirdness had been confined to the village. Maybe they thought they could keep an eye on me here. Or maybe my weirdness simply stood out less among those of the other inhabitants they knew so well.

I smiled and stopped for a moment, taking in the view. The Saône valley stretched out to my right. On a clear day, you could see all the way to Mont Blanc from here. I took another deep breath. I should have brought my camera along – the light was perfect. I squeezed one eye closed as I looked for the right framing of the valley behind my house. Cascading trees on the left, excellent. And the gravel road on the right led the eye straight to... Yuck. Auguste's out-of-use wine tanks – concrete and rusted metal cubes of more than a man's height – were bang in the middle of my composition. I tried moving around a little, but he'd dumped the old *cuves* exactly where they would not be hidden by some well-placed bushes or an overhanging branch. Not even the brambles growing over them would hide them completely.

I stomped my foot on the ground. It was the response of a three-year-old, I knew, but somehow it always calmed me down when there was nothing I could do about whatever was bothering me at the time, and I'd have to let it go. So I turned, rinsed my neighbour's unsightly *cuves* from my brain, and continued my walk.

'*Bonjour, madame.* Going for a baguette?' Monsieur Durand, my neighbour's neighbour, joined me at the end of his lane and gave me his precise smile. Not too friendly, not too distant. Everything about Monsieur Durand was just so. The way he dressed was not too formal, not too casual. His hair was not too stylish, not too old-fashioned. Even his face was not too handsome, not too ugly. He kept everything well under control. I wished him good morning and addressed the issue of the baguette.

'I might as well. See if there's any new gossip about.'

Monsieur Durand lifted an eyebrow. 'I wouldn't have thought you the type.'

'I shouldn't, really. But these village people are just so fascinating. You never know if Marylène will wash those curtains or not. And what if Jean-Baptiste suddenly changes his favourite brand of cigarette?'

He chuckled. 'I see. Life in the city has left you snobbish about us simple country folk.'

'Naturally.' I snorted. Though I liked making fun of village life, there was a reason I'd moved back to it. Village gossip might not be important in the grand scheme of things, but it was mostly innocent and brought a sense of community. The Durands had moved in only a few years ago, after living in Villefranche all their lives. You could live here for twenty years and still be the newcomer, but they'd soon felt at home. All this according to my mother, of course. I hadn't been here to see it, but she was the mayoress. She was supposed to know. At least, again, according to her. Well, what would you expect in a village of less than twelve hundred people?

So whether or not the Durands counted as simple country folk was not my decision to make. Whenever I met Madame Laura Durand in the street, she'd always stop to ask how I was and showed genuine interest in the titbits I offered. But she'd get fidgety after the first few sentences, shuffling her feet and looking down the road to whatever event she was supposedly late for. She was a sweet and soft-spoken woman with a body you could squeeze through a letterbox, and I had the feeling we'd quite like each other if she'd give me the chance. One of these days I'd trick her into having an actual conversation.

As we passed the first houses built in the golden yellow stone that had earned the region its name of Les Pierres Dorées, Monsieur Durand did seem to fit in, though. He strolled along the narrow asphalted pavement, greeting early risers here and there. The council gardeners had parked their water tank on the pavement to tend to the planters that lined the village square, and as we moved around it, Monsieur Durand greeted them by name. My stomach tingled with a hint of jealousy, though I told myself it was hunger. Even before I moved to Villefranche, I'd never known the gardeners' names. I made sure to remember them now. The sturdy, grey-haired one, André. The thin, brown-haired one, Tino.

Across from the church that had always been too big for the size of the congregation, the *boulangerie* overlooked the square, wedged in between the hairdresser's and the butcher's. The ancient wooden beam across the front of the building showed in faded letters the name of the baker's grandfather, along with some of the goodies he'd offered. The same things still on offer today, naturally. Though it was only seven thirty in the morning, we weren't the first customers. Céline, the baker's daughter, was serving an elderly lady with the sweet smile that never seemed to leave her face. I let Monsieur Durand go first while I fought the urge to buy one of those delicious almond croissants. I won, but only barely.

'Madame Belmain here was hoping for some juicy news,' Monsieur Durand announced, handing over the euro twenty-five for his *flûte*.

Céline threw me a sideways glance. 'This is the bakery. You need the butcher's. But they don't open until eight.'

We all laughed politely as Monsieur Durand wished us a good day and left.

'The butcher's doesn't open until eight? Céline, this is news to me. They must have changed their schedule.'

Céline opened her eyes wide. 'Oh yes. In 1943, I believe.' She slid a baguette in a bag for me. 'Oh, now you've got *me* going. I don't even mean it. And I don't believe you do, either. Those few years in the city haven't made you that blasé.'

I tapped my bank card against the machine. 'Honestly, the level of predictability is what drew me back here. No surprises, what you see is what you get. It's a dream.'

Her smile grew wider. 'Enjoy your dream today, Julie.'

The bell over the door jingled when I left with a little wave to Céline.

I shouldn't have, really, but the fresh baguette smelled so good that I ripped off a piece and munched on it on the way back, hoping no one would spot me making this unforgivable transgression of food etiquette. The rising sun promised another glorious autumn day. It probably wouldn't be warm enough for a poolside shoot, but I'd have plenty of warm, natural light in my pictures.

The road leading from the village past my house was not one of the main ones to Villefranche, making it easier to walk alongside it. Passing my brother's house on the right, I came to Auguste's vineyards sloping downward from me on the left. Auguste's land bordered mine, though it enveloped a little plot that held the house belonging to my direct neighbours, the Durands. All three buildings were made of the region's yellow stone, giving them a warm glow even on a grey day, but in direct sunshine, like today, the houses seemed positively edible.

Laura Durand, wrapped as always in several knitted shawls, pulled the front door closed behind her as I passed their property. *'Bonjour!'*

My greeting startled her, but she recovered with a nervous smile and gave me a finger wave. This was not an unusual reaction, but after my earlier musings, I decided it was time to put my resolution into action and have an actual conversation, whether Laura was ready for it or not.

'Lovely day, isn't it?'

She fumbled with her keys. 'Yes... yes.'

I cursed myself for my clumsy opening. Asking generic questions would produce the same casual small talk I got from everyone else in the village. Strangely, the conversations I had with my clients were often more profound than the ones I had with my neighbours. There's something about standing around in frilly granny pants that makes people pass the chitchat stage pretty quickly. The things some people tell me, though, I'd rather not know. 'I love being outside when it's like this. Any special plans for the day?'

'I was just on my way to see Madame Braymand.'

Now that was unusual. Madame Braymand, also known to the locals as La Mademoiselle, lived on her own on the other side of the village and, as far as I knew, had no friends, nor did she want anything to do with anyone else. She was my mother's age, or slightly older, and used to run the post office in the village before they closed it.

'Oh? I didn't know you were friends.'

Her laugh was no more than a puff of air, and paired with the frown, it did not sound joyful at all. 'I wouldn't call us friends per se.' She paused, and ordinarily I would have taken the awkward cue and made my goodbyes, but by now I was determined to have that talk. 'She doesn't have many friends.' Another pause, during which I wondered where this was going. Why would you visit someone you don't seem to like? 'I felt... that someone should do something. About her. About her loneliness. You know?' She looked me in the eye. 'You know.'

And just like that, without even saying much, we'd made a connection. I nodded.

Laura finally relaxed a little. 'It's difficult, isn't it? They all have their own little cliques, the friends they've had for years. If you're not in, you're... out.'

I nodded again. My homecoming had felt like that. Same home, different occupants. Or different me, more accurately. Was I in – or out?

'So I go to her to... sort of... stick together.' Some of her agitation returned when she glanced back at the house. 'Anyway, I should go. I'd better get back before Pierre misses me. It was lovely to see you again.'

Wait! We'd only just started our Actual Conversation. But she'd already turned towards the village.

'If you'd like to come over for an *apéro dinatoire* some time?' It had been years since I'd hosted an *apéro*, a meal at the end of the day consisting of snack-like bites and drinks, but now was as good a time as any to get back in the habit.

She turned with a watery smile. 'Thank you, no. My husband gets anxious around people.'

The man that had said hello to everyone we met on the way?

Laura had continued on her way but slowed down after a few steps and turned back towards me. 'Though... you said you like to be outside? I do go for walks... If you'd want to join me?'

I smiled my broadest smile. 'I'd like that.'

She gave a short nod, pulling on her shawls. 'Nature is good. Nature won't... bother you. I'd better go.'

And with that, she was off. I stared after her, not knowing what to make of our conversation but feeling like I might have just made a slightly odd friend. I wondered what else this day would bring.

2

But it's not even lunchtime

Half an hour later it was time to see what use I could make of my uninvited guest. His bike would allow me to try out some new poses, but I wasn't sure where or how to position it for the best lighting and background. The floor-to-ceiling windows overlooking the garden let in a lot of the morning sun. I might even have to diffuse it with the net curtains I used as a scrim. But if I moved the sofa out of the way, I'd at least have enough space. Whether the bike would work against the flowing white curtains... As I made my way through my studio to the stairs, I considered several other corners of it, but none of them seemed to fit a giant motorcycle.

I halted at the bottom of the staircase and called up. 'Thibault?'

'Come on up.'

'Time to show me what you're made of.'

He waited until I'd climbed the stairs far enough to see him lift his T-shirt. 'Okay.'

'Put that away, you idiot!' Great, now I was blushing. Over a kid! He'd better not get any ideas. 'I don't need to see that. Unless...' Let's see what he'd make of this. 'I can use you for the shoot?'

The T-shirt dropped back down. 'The deal was for my bike.'

Good, situation under control. 'Certainly. So come help me find a good place for it. My client will be here at ten, and I still need to set up the lighting around it. But I won't need you after that.'

He made a face, which annoyed me. He was the one asking me for a favour; he had no right being grumpy about it.

'I know you want to keep an eye on your bike, but this client is one of the more anxious ones. Most get over their hesitation after their initial consultation, but this one was still a little nervous, so I'm not sure how she'll feel about you hanging around.'

'Don't worry, I'm good with nervous women.' He winked at me.

'Thibault...' I groaned.

'What? It's the one thing I do well. I make women feel good.'

'Ugh.' I shook my head, not even wanting to waste words on this.

'Trust me, *mon poussin*,' he said as he came down the stairs, forcing me backwards.

'I am not your chickie,' I protested, but he only laughed.

The bike had better be worth these two days. I made a mental note to ask my client if she would mind a man present at the shoot, and to give Beau a good scowling if he showed when she didn't want him to. My face apparently thought that was a good idea because I found myself scowling at him already.

Making an effort not to be a premature scowler, I pointed at the corner near the back windows. 'Maybe there?'

He wrinkled his nose. 'This place is too white and frilly. Don't you have a garage or something? Or a barn?'

'This is the barn.' I tapped my lip. I'd spent most of my start-up money converting the place and getting rid of as much "authentic" stuff as I could afford. White and frilly was just right for most of my shots, and the rest I shot in the garden, which was also sculpted and manicured into photographic perfection. And now I had to go and bring a man-thing in. Maybe I should just forget about shooting that Harley. But it was rather gorgeous. And it suited my style so well. A simple monochrome backdrop? I could put up a background screen in the garden. That would give me the benefit of the light, but the solid colour might take away from my style.

The sound of Beau's bike made me turn to the side door. He'd gone outside and opened the big wooden doors in the wall linking my house to the studio. From that wall, a slanted roof extended over part of the courtyard, where Beau now parked his Harley. He was right. The bike did not fit in among my white studio furniture. But when he pushed the doors shut, the roofed entrance to the courtyard provided the perfect background. The baby blue paint on the bike contrasted beautifully with the dirty red gravel and the greyish bare wood of the ancient doors.

I believe I may have performed an excited hop, possibly accompanied by a little clap. Though I don't remember doing so, Beau's smug smile said it all.

Straightening my face, I smoothed down my skirt. 'Can you help me take out some reflectors, and probably a scrim, please?'

As expected, Maile's beautiful form appeared at ten to client time. I still couldn't believe my luck in having found her. She looked as if she'd walked straight out of an Elvis-in-Hawaii film: plump red lips, black hair hanging in waves over her shoulders, always wearing bright, flowery pencil skirts over her gorgeous curves. She made all her own clothes and was responsible for most of the items in my wardrobe, both my professional and my private one. The mix of Dior's New Look and rockabilly might not be all that fashionable in France right now, but a pencil skirt looks great on figures that don't actually resemble a pencil. And my love of chocolate chip cookies would always set me apart from the standard French figure.

On top of that, she was a magician with make-up, cutting down significantly on my editing time. Everyone can *look* pretty, but some people require more assistance to *feel* pretty. Maile had a gift for making women feel at ease and bringing out their confidence, something I had first-hand experience with. Only after I'd told Maile all about my history did I find out she was married to Thibault's best friend Gío, who owned the motorcycle shop in Villefranche that they lived above. She'd felt obliged to tell me that, but never mentioned anything to do with Beau or his family afterwards. Today, however, I might press her on that subject.

'Hi, Juju. What's on the menu for this one?'

'I wanted to start off with "Swing It" and maybe "Hold the Phone" or "Hooked". But I also have Thibault's Harley to work with, so maybe—'

'Beau lent you his bike?' Maile looked shocked, which I thought was odd – I'd expected her to know all about Beau's 'escape'.

'No, I traded the use of it for letting him stay here.' When that didn't clear up the confusion on her face, I narrowed my eyes. Clearly, I was not the last person he'd asked for help. If Thibault hadn't appeared at the top of the stairs, I would have shared my concern with her. Now it would have to wait. 'Never mind. I'll need a red dress to complement the baby blue. But I'll have to experiment with poses.'

When Beau joined us, Maile sent him a bunch of unsubtly questioning looks. His eyes flicked from her to me and back, and he held his palms up.

I sighed. 'Would you two like me to leave you alone?'

Maile reddened and disappeared to the dressing room. Beau gave me the same palms-up gesture.

I held up my mother finger. 'I'm on to you. Stay out of sight.'

So of course he stood next to me when my client walked in, looking even more nervous than before. She was forty-four and hoping to surprise her husband with some cheeky pictures of herself because, in her words, he thought her sexier than she thought herself. I was here to remedy that, although she didn't know it yet.

'Agathe, good to see you. This is Thibault, my assistant.'

Beau shook her hand with no more than a warm smile. So far so good.

'Don't worry, though. I will absolutely send him away if you'd prefer a girls-only shoot.' When she sized him up, not giving me a yes or no, I added, 'At any time.'

I talked her through the poses I'd selected for her, which she agreed with, and by the time she went in to Maile, she'd calmed considerably. We'd do the motorcycle shots first, so that if Agathe wanted Beau gone after all, he wouldn't have to worry about his precious bike. But when I came to collect her from Maile, I found a changed woman.

'Look how pretty I am!' She beamed at me.

I smiled. 'I know. That's what your husband sees all the time.'

She said nothing but turned back to the mirror. Mission accomplished. I mouthed 'good work' to Maile, and got Agathe out of there before she could tear up and ruin her make-up. Beau was waiting outside, giving Agathe a wolf whistle when he saw her. She giggled, but then some of the worry returned to her face.

'What if all this doesn't come through in the pictures?'

I wanted to reassure her, but Beau stepped in. 'You don't need to worry about that. You are shining today.' He gave her an intense look that would have made me shiver if it weren't for his smile. Agathe didn't seem certain what to make of him either, judging by the nervous laugh that escaped. I'd better make this quick.

'Agathe, can you get on the motorcycle, please?'

She touched the saddle, but made no attempt to get on. 'Is it yours?' she asked Beau.

He smirked. 'Yes, so you'd better take good care of her. Here, let me help you. Lift your leg. Other leg, *ma chèvre*.'

I froze. What was he doing? You don't call a woman twice your age your goat! Agathe blinked twice, then burst out laughing. Somehow, Beau had broken the ice, and everything went smoothly from then on. She didn't send him away and talked animatedly about her children and her husband, and how she'd thought about doing this shoot for a very long time before giving in.

The red dress with cap sleeves was the perfect colour for her, and the puffy petticoat gave her a floaty appearance, enhanced by the fact that she kept playing with it. Most women aren't used to having a wide skirt any more, so when they lower their hands and encounter their skirt, the playing comes naturally. I gave her a wrench and told her to sit beside the motorcycle. 'Turn this way and bend your right knee. No, leave the skirt. It's supposed to show your garter, remember?'

She grinned at me through the camera, and I clicked because she looked radiant. Before I could get her to act surprised, though, her mouth was working again. Now it was a story about her cat. Agathe had come to me through one of my other clients. Both of them lived in Pruniers, a village some miles to the south-east. Born and bred, left only for college in Lyon. If I had done that, how different would my life have been? I never did go to college, much to my mother's dismay. My dad had been fine with my decision, as long as I worked instead. So I did. Worked my way up in the make-up department of a large store. And then I met Franck. Ugh, time to stop this train of thought.

Agathe had started a story about her friends. I tried to get in there to direct her, but although she did as I told her, none of it stopped her from talking. It seemed her reserves had been thoroughly put aside, and she was enjoying herself to the fullest. Beau got lucky this time, but I'd have to tell him off later. His goat, of all things!

For the next scene we went into the garden, where I'd hung a large swing from an old tree. Perfect for having the wind blow up skirts. Agathe's rosy cheeks made for gorgeous pictures. It was hard to get her to make a surprised face for the photo, she was smiling so much. I settled for a saucy look, which I was sure would delight her husband.

The rest of the shoot passed quickly, though a drink of water made for the only respite from Agathe's babbling. I smiled along politely for most of it but did feel a little proud when she said goodbye with the words, 'This was the most fun I've had since my wedding day.' I promised her the photos would be ready within a week and closed the door behind her with a little sigh of relief.

Silence.

'Hey.'

I jumped. No more silence. For a blissful moment, I'd forgotten about Beau.

'Whoa. Heavy conscience? I only wanted to ask if you need help fixing *déjeuner*?'

Not really. I always cooked two portions, but they normally lasted me as many days. As long as he offered, though...

'Can you make a roux?'

'Hey, I may be blond, but I'm still French.'

Before I could answer, my phone vibrated on my desk. It had been doing so on and off, but I made it a point never to check my phone while I was with a client. 'Hang on, it's my best friend. She doesn't usually call on my working days. Tiana? Something wrong?'

'Where have you been?! Someone killed La Mademoiselle.'

'But it's not even lunch time.'

My friend had no answer to that at first. After a few seconds she said, 'That makes no sense.'

By then my brain had kicked in. 'Sorry. Your words sounded like an accusation, and my first instinct was to defend. Who would kill La Mademoiselle? I mean, she could get really nasty, but I think she was just miserable after they closed her beloved post office. So... why?'

'They don't know!' Tiana sounded more excited than she had in years. She was usually the quiet, thoughtful one. 'The whole village is talking about it, even though nobody knows a thing, of course. I've already heard three different theories.'

That was more like the cynical tone I'd expected. The shock of the news must have shown on my face because Thibault was staring at me with a mix of worry and curiosity. I covered my phone to explain. 'There's been a murder in the village.'

'Whoa!' It came out through a big smile, which transferred the worry to me. 'I thought it would be boring to live in a village, but that's awesome. Who is it?'

'You don't know her.' My already serious doubts about letting him stay were not far away from turning into certainty after that reaction.

'Who are you talking to? Is that a man?' Tiana demanded to know.

'Hardly. Do they know who did it?'

'No. It's all very mysterious. So far, I've heard drugs, blackmail, and buried treasure.'

'Buried... What?!'

'Well, that one came from Isabel Cochon, so, you know... Grains of salt and all that.'

That explained it. The butcher's wife always had the most outrageous stories to share. But sometimes they turned out to be true. Buried treasure, though...

'Right. I suppose it's as good an explanation as any. I can't think of any motive that would make sense.'

'Oh, yes, I can totally see La Mademoiselle as a pirate. Or a smuggler. Have you completely lost it, Juju?'

'No, no, not like that. More like, if she had something valuable that's been stolen?'

'That's what people call robbery, you know. Not buried treasure. But, apparently, there weren't any signs of forced entry, as they call it on TV.'

One dazzlingly implausible theory after another formed in my head, as Beau was waving at me for more details. 'But... she wasn't rich... or powerful... or involved in anything, really. She was just some old lady shouting at children playing too loudly for her liking. It's so strange.'

'Isn't it? Anyway, I thought you'd want to know. I'd better get back to my other distractions. These kissing books won't write themselves.'

'How can you think of romance when someone has been murdered? In our village!'

'Mmm, yes, I would prefer to go to my weeping parlour. Unfortunately, I need money to buy food. Since my money comes from my books, I need to actually write them first. Let me know if you figure out who did it!'

She'd hung up before I could tell her I wasn't going to go anywhere near a dead person. She'd known me all my life. She should know that.

Beau was still in my face, practically bursting with impatience. 'So? Who was it?'

'I told you, you wouldn't know her.'

'No, I mean who did it? Or was it just gang violence?'

Frowning, I pushed past him out of my office and crossed the courtyard to my house. 'You say that as if that would be less bad than some other kind of murder.'

He followed me with stars in his eyes. 'Not that, but less interesting.'

I stopped on the threshold and he almost bumped into me. 'Are you serious? Gang violence in a small village and with an old lady as the victim? Beau, this is a grave matter. A little more respect is in order.'

'Sure, *bien sûr*.' He didn't look more respectful in any way. 'Did you know her?'

Shrugging, I entered the house and installed myself on Aunt Geraldine's lush grey sofa. It was the most modern item of furniture she had possessed and by far the most comfortable. But it had been too big for her new apartment, so she'd had to leave it. I gave her some extra money for it, but nothing like its true value. Brushing my hand over the soft fabric, I answered Thibault's question.

'Not really. She used to run the Saint-Maurice post office before they closed it. It was the place to be when I was little. La Mademoiselle... Claire Braymand. In spite of its grammatical incorrectness and the fact that the term had been abolished in official use years ago, everyone called her La Mademoiselle because she was very proud of the fact that she'd put her work before everything else, including her love life. She talked to everyone and always remembered to ask about what they'd told her previously. But then five years ago, they closed the branch and retired her. She became a bit of a recluse, never talking to anyone any more except to screech from behind the door to leave her alone. I just don't get why anyone would want to kill her. She was pretty much the most boring person in the village.'

'So they don't know who killed her?' He finally seemed to put some more thought into his attitude. My description had made her a real person, losing a real life, as dull as it might have been.

I held my palms up just as the cat flap let in Henri. He wasn't my cat. He wasn't anyone's cat. But he lived in my garden part-time, and last summer while my house and studio were being renovated, he often came and jumped in my lap when I was enjoying my new garden on a Sunday afternoon. After three times, I had them install a cat flap. At first, Henri only used it to escape when I took him into the house, but as soon as I put down a bowl of cat food, my house became his.

Henri now jumped on my lap as usual, waiting for me to start absent-mindedly stroking him. He knew instinctively when I needed to think and came in for a cuddle at the exact right time. Sometimes I didn't see him for days, but as soon as I sat down for a good reflection on whatever was bugging me, there he was.

'You're not telling me I moved to the one village in the Beaujolais that houses a demented killer, right?'

'Oh, so you've moved here now, have you? But if there is a demented killer, they seem to be targeting old ladies. I think you're in the clear.'

'Good, then I'll get started on lunch.'

'Thanks to you, we finished early today. I'll hop to the butcher's in a minute, but you should spend your time finding out where you'll "move to" in two days.'

He spread his arms wide as if to say that was a problem for future Thibault, turned, and disappeared out the door.

I scratched Henri's head. Thibault might have shrugged the news off lightly, but I was not so lucky. Why hadn't Céline said anything earlier today? Not wanting to gossip was one thing, but news of a murder must have reached the bakery almost instantly at that time of day. Especially one so baffling. She must not have known.

Wait. Laura Durand was on her way to see La Mademoiselle. She must have been the one who found her. Poor soul.

I lifted the little *tigré* in my lap, so I could look him in the eye. 'So who did it, Henri? Huh? Do you know?'

Henri hated when I did that. He jumped across the room and sprinted through the cat flap as soon as I put him down. He was free to do as he pleased. As hard as I'd worked to be free myself, I didn't feel like I was. I sighed. Alone again. Like

La Mademoiselle. That thought sent an actual shiver down my spine. Maybe having Thibault here right now wasn't so bad after all? Hm. I'd worked hard to have my own space. My own village, my own studio, my own house. Having someone else here, especially a *man*, meant relinquishing some of that safety. I mean freedom!

Sighing again, I got up. Alone was good. Alone was in control. Except when someone murdered you. But who would murder me? Then again, who would murder her? She had her groceries delivered and generally kept herself to herself. A far cry from all those years ago at the post office.

I used to have lots of friends. Before I left. Before Franck. A far cry from where I was now...

With a deep breath, I repeated the gesture I'd made so many times before, putting my thumb and index finger to my forehead and pulling, as if plucking something from my head. Negativity, out. I was not going to be like her. I was going out right now, to show that killer I still got my own groceries. If that didn't deter them from killing me, I didn't know what would.

3

Go introduce yourself!

Tiana Lebrun was supposed to be writing. Like she'd told her best friend, someone had to make the money to put food on the table. And since she lived alone, that someone was her. But come on, a person had been murdered! Talk about killing your creativity. Well, that's what she'd say to anyone who'd ask. Not that anyone would. But in reality, a murder in your immediate surroundings is not something you shake off that easily. Whether you liked the person or not.

Her gaze drifted from the computer screen out the window. Big mistake. She didn't have time for that particular distraction. She picked up her phone and took a picture, feeling like a creepy stalker doing it, but hey, he was out there in the open, for all the world to see. Why not show him to a bit of the rest of the world?

Tiana sent her fellow writers the picture over the group chat.

Tiana: *Guys, this is my neighbours' new gardener. How am I ever going to get any work done?*

The others didn't take long.

Teddy: *Squee!*

Rachel: *I love brunos! Brunets? What's the male version of a brunette?*

Carole: *Does he always work shirtless??*

Sophia: *Is that a mermaid tattoo?*

Elizabeth: *Hang on, coming over right now! I don't care that you're in another country!*

Predictable as the reactions from a bunch of romance writers to a picture of a muscular torso might be, they still made Tiana smile. She glanced from her bedroom window into the neighbours' garden. Yep, still shirtless. Still gorgeous. He should be excellent inspirational material, but instead, he was just distracting.

Tiana: *I'm going to need to buy some new undies if he's going to be out there, looking at my laundry.*

Another wave of choking, fainting and otherwise mortified emojis followed.

Teddy: *Go introduce yourself!*

Extroverts shouldn't be allowed to be writers. Teddy simply had no idea.

Rachel: *In this case, I think I might agree.*

Rachel?! How could she? Before any of the others chimed in, Tiana put her phone down and went back to her computer screen. *Write, girl. That's what you're supposed to do.* Hands hovering above the keyboard, she sighed. *Okay, maybe just one more little peek.*

She planted her elbows on her desk and let her face drop to her palms. This was so bad! Perhaps she should just go and return that plate to her neighbour. The biscuits were long gone and she'd been meaning to return it for a while now. What better opportunity to face her distraction, right?

On her way out she checked the mirror. Striking. That's what people called her. It wasn't exactly 'pretty', but she'd take it. Green eyes weren't as common in real life as they were in romance novels, but she had them, a greyish shade of jade that stood out against her light brown skin and dark brown hair. The total package was, well, striking.

Would the neighbours' hot new gardener go for striking? Maybe she should fill the plate with biscuits again. But *obviously* she didn't have any biscuits, because *obviously* she hadn't done any shopping, because *obviously* she'd been lost in her stories again. Tiana sighed. Before she could climb back into bed and lament her lack of courage, she went out and knocked on her neighbours' door.

A bubbly woman in her early sixties, with a short, bubbly figure to match, opened the door almost instantly.

'Isn't he gorgeous?' Count on Catherine to come to the point. 'I was wondering if I should invite you, but I see you've found an excuse.'

Really, why would anyone bother talking to Catherine? She would always arrive at the right conclusion before anyone had said anything. Not even murder in the village could deter Cat from her goal. 'Hi, Cat. Here's your plate.'

'Come in, come in, come in.' She almost dragged Tiana towards the kitchen, where they had the best view of the garden. Banzaï, Catherine's massive golden Labrador, harrumphed and relocated to a quieter part of the house. Sweet white coffee appeared magically in Tiana's hands after she'd taken a seat at the kitchen counter. Cat was one of those super-social people who had at least two different visitors each day and still remembered how all her hundreds of friends and acquaintances liked their coffee, or if they preferred tea. She didn't even have to think about it, already peering through the windows, ogling her new toy.

Tiana hid a smile in her coffee cup. Cat was harmless enough. Her long-time, long-suffering boyfriend, Daniel, bumbled in to fill his coffee cup. He shook his head at Cat's back, winked at Tiana, and turned to leave.

'I saw that!' Cat probably knew it more than she'd seen it, but these two were too well-matched to mind each other's quirks. 'Soooo...' Cat tore herself away from the window and faced Tiana. 'What do you think?'

Tiana blushed and made a series of non-committal noises with accompanying gestures.

'Oh, please! You write romance novels. He could be on your cover! Here, let me call him inside.'

Panic! 'Nononon—'

Catherine had already opened the kitchen door. 'Lucas! D'you want some coffee?'

Tiana groaned. Eyes wide, and now brushing at a brand new coffee stain down her front, she did a quick mental search. She had not had enough time to think about what she was going to say to him when she met him. Maybe she could let Catherine do the talking. What was the standard small talk for meeting handsome, muscular— Oh gosh, his smile was mouth-watering.

'Lucas, this is Tiana, my neighbour. She writes romance novels. I was just telling her to put you on the cover. Everyone would buy it!'

Cat's kitchen had never been this warm before. Tiana's cheeks felt so hot, she was sure they emitted light. The things that woman said! And got away with... Lucas, regrettably with his shirt back on, grinned and nudged Catherine's shoulder with his elbow. They were pretty much at the same height. Tiana's ballooning insides deflated a little when Lucas didn't seem to take offence at Cat's words, but her cheeks still radiated when he held out his hand. The mermaid's tail peeked out from under his sleeve.

'Hi, nice to meet you.'

'You too.' Should she apologise for what Cat had said? It felt like she should say something. Something more than just 'you too'. Now would be the time to say that something. Oh gosh, too late. If she apologised now, it would just be awkward. Maybe say something else?

'So you're a writer. Have you written many books yet?'

Still rummaging in her mental box of awkward small talk, Tiana needed a split second to realise he'd said something. What did he say? A question. One she could actually answer, yay!

'Twelve. Twelve finished ones. Published, I mean.' A stupid little breathy giggle escaped. She clutched her coffee cup with both hands and took a sip, just to have an excuse not to say any more.

Lucas made the appropriate impressed face. 'Twelve, wow. You must have started young. Or write really quickly.'

'I'm older than I look.' Aaand the cheek radiation was back.

'What she means is,' Catherine intervened, 'she's that good. On paper, that is. In person, you'll have to get to know her better to get more words out of her. But I don't think that'll be a problem. I'll think of more things I want changed around the garden.'

Lucas's laugh resounded through the kitchen, while Tiana tried her best to melt into the floor. To no avail. She was still here. Darn. She loved Cat, and she didn't mind being the butt of her jokes in private, but in front of someone she'd really like to get to know? *Oh well, there's that chance shot.* At least now she could try to focus on her writing again. So maybe Cat's inappropriateness was a blessing in disguise. Tiana might make that deadline after all.

She zoned out while Cat and Lucas flirted, trying to remember where she'd left off with her latest story. But even that didn't work. Miserable situation. She emptied her cup and made a feeble excuse.

'Yeah, I'm going to take off too.' Lucas drained his cup and put it on the counter. 'I'll see you after lunch, Cat.'

'All right.' Cat hopped on a bar stool and left them to find their own way out.

Once outside, Tiana hesitated. Should she apologise? It wasn't really her fault. Still, not saying anything felt wrong too.

'I'm sorry about that.'

Wait, that wasn't her voice. What was he apologising for? She looked up at his brown eyes, not knowing what to say. Again.

'For letting Catherine make fun of you, I mean.'

Oh. Tiana shrugged. 'She means well.'

'She's not the most diplomatic of people, though.'

That made her laugh. And with that laugh, her tension fell away. She even dared to look at him without blushing. They'd arrived at her door. Now would be a good time to say something clever.

Lucas gave her a little wave. 'See you later?'

She nodded. Nothing clever came out. It didn't matter.

4

A perm like that never looked good on anyone

As this morning's shoot had gone so smoothly, I had a little time to kill before lunch. Just enough for a quick visit to the butcher's. I remembered that Thibault liked *saucisson sec*, a dried sausage I detested and thus did not have in the house. And though I didn't want him there, I was raised to be a good hostess. On my way to buy the abominable sausage for my unwanted guest, I cursed my perfect upbringing. But as the village's most high-profile family, there was no getting away from the perfect upbringing. That church I mentioned? Donated by one of my ancestors. That castle higher up the hill? We're related to the *vicomtesse*, somewhere in the distant past. Still, don't think I have any illusions of grandeur. Only twelve hundred people in this village, remember?

Warm autumn air filled with various scents of lunches being cooked filled my nostrils and made my stomach growl. I waited for it to stop before I entered the not unpleasant chill of the butcher's shop. One other woman had decided to buy her meat last minute. Madame Dufaux had kept her maiden name when she married Monsieur Vray and the village was still talking about it. She was one of those people that never seem old or young, but she must have been in her thirties, judging from her husband's age. Madame Dufaux adored her husband, but she always complained about him. 'He doesn't know his sheets from his blankets, but he's a good man.' That kind of thing.

She was finishing up when I came in, greeting me with a pleasant smile. She had a freshness about her that made her look pretty, even if her features themselves were nothing special. But the unruly frizz on her head... I was dying to send her to Maile and make her see what a beauty she could be. But then, not everyone cares about that. I gave her a warm smile in return and turned to Isabel, who tutted as Madame Dufaux left the shop.

'A perm like that never looked good on anyone.' Ah yes, Isabel Cochon, the butcher's wife, who always had an opinion ready. Céline had been right this morning when she said that one needs the butcher's for gossip. Neither Isabel nor her husband Charles held back when it came to unofficial news. Where she gave it over the counter, he spread the word while making deliveries in his van, flashy sunglasses on his nose, a big cigar between his teeth, and soothing classical music blasting at full volume from the speakers.

I blinked twice and proceeded with my order. This village. You can know everyone, and still be astonished by them.

'I assume you've heard about the murder?' Isabel continued as if she hadn't just burned down her other client.

I nodded and braced myself.

'I reckon someone bumped her off to steal her treasure,' she said, as if that sort of thing happened every day around here.

'I didn't know she had any.' Trying to stay as neutral as possible was probably best in this situation.

'She probably didn't herself. You see...' She balanced her ample bosom on the display counter as she leaned forward. 'I think her house was on an old smugglers' route. If you ask me, someone's just been released from prison and came for his loot.'

Wow. Someone had been reading too many boys' books. 'Do you have any reason for thinking that?' I couldn't help myself.

She stepped back as though I'd offended her. 'What other reason could anyone have for murdering an old woman?'

What reason indeed? I made a non-committal gesture, bagged my sausage, and bid her good day. I'd survived another social encounter.

Cooking with Thibault was a surprisingly relaxed affair. We quickly fell into the banter we used to enjoy years ago as we moved around the kitchen, which was furnished with marble-topped wooden cabinets. Other than my sleek, white studio with its bright accents, my house was filled with natural materials and soft colours. I had upgraded my aunt's *déco* and framed part of my collection of keys – mostly the antique, pretty ones – but the old-fashioned cosiness of the place remained.

At a silence in our conversation, Beau switched on the radio and hummed along until the refrain. Then he belted out, 'I tested drains down in Ahaaafrica.'

I stared at him.

'What?'

But before I could comment on his... creativity, he jumped back from the pan and shook his hand vigorously. Maybe I should have warned him that pan's handle got really hot, but in my defence, he distracted me with his singing.

'Grab your earlobe,' I advised him.

'What?'

'Just do it.'

The gesture was more than a little hesitant. 'Hey, it works!'

'Stick with me, you'll learn things.' I shrugged. 'Something to do with blood circulation, I believe. Takes the excess heat out of a burned fingertip.'

'How can I stick with you if you want me out the day after tomorrow?'

'Figure of speech.'

I took two plates from the cupboard and showed him where to get the cutlery and the wine glasses. As we sat down to a light pumpkin soup, I asked, 'So are you going to tell me—'

'Nope.'

Though that was to be expected, and I trusted him to tell me when he was ready, I couldn't help wondering what had happened that had finally driven him to leave. He loved his shady family, though as far as I knew he'd always refused to take part in their business. So what could have caused him to call his departure an escape? And would they be coming after him? That made my stomach contract. I did not need my ex-in-laws stomping all over my safe space. Perhaps Maile would know more.

Glancing at Thibault, I thought that was that, and I'd ruined the atmosphere, but he went on, 'How about you?'

'What do you mean?'

'Well, I haven't seen you in five years. I mean, I sort of heard your story through Maile and Gío, but...'

I shrugged. 'Not much else to tell. Franck used my beauty blog to cover up his own business. When I found out, I divorced him, but then, instead of just using me, he actually targeted my blog. So I helped put him in jail. End of story.'

He knew all that. It was his family we were talking about, and they were a pretty close-knit bunch. A tiny voice inside me asked whether he could have continued in the family tradition after all, but I told it to be quiet. This was Beau, not Franck. Still, I'd take extra precautions to keep him away from my clients' personal and financial information, just to be sure.

'And four years later you just happen to own a well-running photography business.'

I shrugged again, standing to take the celery, apple, and mushroom salad and the grilled chicken to the table. What did he want from me? Details of all the tears and frustration that had come from a life with Franck? Specifics of how he'd ruined my sanity? Charm ran in this family, and after my father died, Franck seemed to be exactly what I needed: debonair and handsome, he swept me off my feet with promises of undying love and devotion. But he'd made me choose between him and my family when I was still too smitten to realise there would be no way back. Slowly cut me off from the outside world while claiming to protect me from a family that didn't appreciate my dissimilarity. Not only had he wrecked my business, but he'd destroyed my friendships, my hopes, and my confidence on his way down.

What would Maile have told Thibault? She'd only met me two years ago. She didn't see the lonely skeleton I had become years before, wearing nothing but joggers and sitting on the couch all day, staring into nothingness, jumping at every little sound. She hadn't lived through the pain of hitting rock bottom and seeing no way up.

My mother had saved me. I hadn't dared contact anyone from my old life after I'd been so rude to them under Franck's influence, but she had been relentless in her search for me, pulling every political string she could reach. And finally standing outside my flat for hours, talking, while I was too scared to open the door.

After a few weeks, I'd worked up enough courage to call Tiana. She'd hugged me for what felt like an hour, crying with me and holding me till neither of us had any tears left. But that was the moment a little light sparked inside. If there were no tears left, maybe there was hope for me after all. Maybe even laughter. It had taken a long time, but I'd worked hard, and, with the help of my mother and friend, ended up in a place of my choosing. If Thibault had any hopes of staying even for two days, he'd better not upset my chosen place.

Fortunately, he saw that too, chatting instead about how he'd been working in Gío's motorcycle shop for a while, but he'd wanted a break from it. I guessed that's where Beau's bike came from, although I still wondered whether he could have afforded it on the salary Gío would have paid him.

By the time we'd finished our spiced pears, I'd at least decided what Thibault would be good for.

'You do the dishes, all right?'

He gave me a sour look but began clearing away. As I retreated to my living room, my phone rang.

'Hi, *maman*, you're early.' She always called me on Wednesday evenings. Why, I'd no idea, but she liked to stick to schedules. I relaxed onto the couch and put my feet up.

'I know, but I think my day is going to be completely filled up. Can you imagine? Murder! In my village!' She was only the mayor, but she talked as if the village was her property. Fortunately, she didn't rule it as such, so everyone forgave her this little quirk. Some even considered it endearing, and called her the Mother of the Village. 'Anyway, how are you?'

'Oh, I'm fi—'

'You wouldn't have an idea of who could have done such a thing, would you?'

She knew I'd be fine. What could possibly have happened to me that was more important than a murder in her village, right? '*Maman*, I hardly know anyone around here any more. Especially not anyone who would take another's life. I make it a point to avoid those people.'

'Hmm, well, you never know, do you? Poor Madame Durand.'

So I'd been correct, it was Laura who'd found her. It must have been a horrible shock. I'd better go over there in a bit, see if I could help her in any way. I gave my mother my condolences, as Madame Braymand had once been if not a friend, then at least someone she was relatively close to. But my mother took an unforgiving stance.

'Nobody deserves to be murdered, but she had long since forgotten how to be anybody's friend. I don't expect many people to come to the funeral, except maybe one or two whose curiosity gets the better of them.'

I wished my mother good luck with all the paperwork and hung up, staring at the wall. How sad, to have so few people left in your life that, even when it's taken from you in such a violent way, nobody seems to care much. I stood and grabbed my purse. The one thing I could do was show support to the living.

'My next client will be here at two thirty, so I'm just going to nip next door to my neighbour to see how she's doing. She found the murdered woman,' I explained to Thibault. 'Good luck with the house hunting!' I threw over my shoulder as I pulled the door shut.

I knocked on my neighbour's door, not really expecting to be admitted. But when Monsieur Durand opened the door, he was just as calm and composed as ever.

'Madame Belmain.'

'Good... afternoon. I've come to see Laura?'

'Yes, of course. Do come in.' He waved me in, passing the kitchen and a small study, to the lounge room at the back, but hesitated in inviting me to sit down. 'I'll notify her.'

He left me without an explanation, so I sat down and waited.

It took ten minutes for someone to come in, and by then I'd almost resorted to counting stones in the wall I could see through the window. The room's décor was minimalist to say the least. A couch, a coffee table, two big, comfortable chairs. One potted plant in the corner, a black-and-white photograph on the mantle, and one ceramic figurine. Those were the entire contents of the room. I wondered for half a second if they didn't have much money, but I was sure Monsieur Durand had a good job, and this house must not have been cheap either.

My thoughts were interrupted by a light cough. Laura Durand's deep-set eyes avoided me, while her shaking hands held on to her husband. Letting go of him, she shuffled around, straightening the two trinkets, and didn't answer my greeting.

'How are you?' Wildly inadequate, but I had to start somewhere.

A barely there shrug. Monsieur Durand led his wife to one of the chairs, straightened her knit shawl, and whispered something to her that sounded like 'keep it together'. As soon as he left the room, however, she let out a faltering breath that ended in a sob.

'I'm sorry,' she said softly. 'I do try to be strong.'

My heart went out to her. 'Don't worry about it. Is there anything I can do?'

This evoked the thinnest of smiles. She gave a tiny shake of her head but seemed to calm down a little. The slight hunch she always had was more pronounced now, emphasising her gaunt frame.

'You must have had a terrible shock.'

The woman in front of me, though jittery at the best of times, had lost all her usual attentive friendliness. She looked up, her dark eyes piercing mine. The anguish pouring out of them was a clear cry for help that surprised and shook me. 'Oh Julie, it was awful.'

I got up and knelt at her side.

'So awful!' She buried her face in her hands, silently sobbing.

Searching for anything to say, I put my hand on her knee and rubbed her back.

'I couldn't... I can't...'

With a soothing 'shhh' I tried to calm her. 'You don't have to say anything.'

She jerked her hands down and straightened, pinning me with that dark stare. 'Yes, I do. I have to.' But as she looked at me, her resolve melted away and she cowered once more, dropping her gaze to the hands in her lap. 'So awful,' she whispered.

The poor woman was trembling under my hands, and I still couldn't find the words to help her.

'Have you talked to anyone?'

Her response was half-nod, half head-shake. 'They sent someone round. She was nice enough, but she couldn't help me.' Tears brimmed in her eyes again. 'No one can help me, Julie. I tried to help myself, and look what happened!'

She took a few deep breaths, faltering at first but steadier as she went on, until she seemed to have regained some control. 'I went to Madame Braymand's house this morning, as I always do. I let myself in with the key she gave me, but when I called out, she didn't answer. When I saw the chaos in the salon, my first thought was that she was robbed, but then I found the body.' She shuddered. 'I ran out and screamed for help. Someone must have called the police, but I don't remember much after that.'

It came out rehearsed and mechanical, but Madame Durand took obvious pride in having delivered her message, so I smiled in what I hoped was an encouraging way, without pity. 'It's good that Madame Braymand had you in her life. She didn't seem to have many others she could rely on.'

'No...' She paused. 'There was of course Madame Madora – Marie. They used to be friends, long ago. You know, when the post office was still open and Madame Braymand reigned over it. But they hadn't spoken in years. I think.'

'Madora... That's the German couple, right?'

'Dutch. They must have already been here before you left, don't you remember?'

My cheeks heated. I did know, but at the time, my thoughts were on other matters. And it was nine years ago. 'I saw her the other day, taking her kids to school.' In fact, I saw her quite often. The mother of three boys, who made up for the lack of princesses around her by dressing like one. It made her look like Snow White surrounded by at least three dwarves – more if the boys had friends over. Of course, those boys weren't here when I left.

'Yes... Another import. You know how it is. She's settled well, though. And so nice.' She prattled on more quickly, as if on an accelerating autopilot, staring at the wringing hands in her lap. 'So nice. I really shouldn't... She must be relieved too. But I can't. I have to...' She bit her lip and shivered. 'I'd like to rest now. Thank you for coming.'

Her voice had gone flat again. I wished there was something I could do, but she clearly wanted me out, so I rose with some empty words of solace. I turned, but before I could leave, her thin hand gripped my arm.

'Julie, do you... Do you think I'm a bad person?'

Now where did that come from? 'No, of course not. You were the only one who still cared for La Mademoiselle.'

She wrung her hands, her gaze darting left and right. 'Yes, but... I didn't... really. In a way, I'm glad that I... that she's dead.' Her eyes fixed on me with a pleading expression. 'Does that make me horrible?'

With a slight smile I put a hand on her arm. 'You've had a nasty shock, but trust me – nobody would even think to call you horrible.'

She seemed to relax a little after that. Curious sentiment. Why would she continue her visits to La Mademoiselle if she didn't like her? But if she did it out of a sense of duty, the death must have also brought some relief, which was probably what she felt guilty about. But that did not make her a bad person. Poor thing.

5

You think it's creepy?

Opposite the houses of Auguste and the Durands was a communal block of letterboxes. Our little street only had three: Auguste's, the Durands', and mine. Out of habit, whenever I passed it, I checked my letterbox, although it hadn't contained any fun surprises yet. Just bills. Today, it contained a simple white envelope with no mark on it, not even a name. I closed the letterbox with a slight frown, turning the envelope over in my hands as I returned to my own front door.

'Intriguing,' I mumbled to the lion's head doorknob. But when I unfolded the plain white sheet of paper inside, my eyes bulged. Was it even for me? A quick check. The letter was addressed to Julie Belmain. Yep, that would be me.

I crushed the paper into a ball and scowled at it, my blood pressure rising. Taking a deep breath, I put my thumb and index finger to my forehead and pulled the negativity out, depositing the imaginary filth outside the door. I'd just leave that there.

Entering the kitchen, I threw the wad in the paper bin. And that was that. No more nasty letter. Hardly a letter at all. Seven measly words. 'Julie Belmain, I know about your husband.'

I sat down at the kitchen table and picked up a leaflet for something or other. After having stared at it for two minutes, though, I still had no idea what it was for. My eye kept wandering to the corner of my kitchen where the recycling bins lived. In my head, that crumpled letter was a strange link to the murdered woman. Who would send something like that? Everyone in the village knew who I'd been married to, didn't they? I fished it out of the bin and smoothed it out, just as Thibault entered. Had I not locked the door to the courtyard?

'Reading old love letters again? Juju, that time has passed. You should simply accept it and move on.' He turned to cut himself a piece of *saucisson*. Had we not finished lunch half an hour ago? How could he be hungry again?

I shook my head, letting the not-up-to-standard remark pass. 'Not a love letter, and not old. Found this in my letterbox just now.' I handed him the sheet of paper, which he took as he sat down.

'I know about your husband. Doesn't everyone?'

'That's what I thought. So why would anyone take the trouble to write me a creepy letter about it?'

He looked me in the eye. 'You think it's creepy?'

'Well...' Did I? I really didn't want him to think I didn't feel safe. He might use it as an excuse to stay. 'I'm sure it's just someone's idea of a prank. An unsigned letter like this would be creepy, but since it's such a hollow statement, I'd already thrown it away.'

'Then why were you looking at it now?'

He slid the paper back to me, and I smoothed it out again.

'I don't know. Because of the murder, I suppose.'

The hand with another piece of sausage paused on its way to his mouth. 'What does that have to do with your letter?'

'Oh, just because it's a letter, you know, and she used to run the post office. I'm sure there's no actual connection.'

'But you've no idea who could have sent it, even as a joke?' he asked between chews.

'Not a clue.' I stared at him, then at the paper. I slammed my hand down on the sheet and crumpled it again. 'And that's too much time I've spent on it already.' I stood and threw the ball back into the bin. 'I have work to do.'

'Call me if you need me.' He took a little pad out of his back pocket and started drawing. I'd forgotten he did that, getting so engrossed in his art that he wouldn't even have heard me if I'd answered. I left him there for now, as I still had my rounds to do, going over what sets and props I'd be using and checking my lighting.

Maile's arrival signalled ten minutes and counting, but I wanted a moment to talk to her.

'Not much to do on this one, is there?' she asked, hanging her bag from a peg on the back of the door.

'So you didn't know Beau had fled the family?'

She blinked at my directness, then gave a non-committal shrug and turned to the clothes rack. 'Not the first time he's tried.'

'Maile...' Why was this so difficult? 'He's not... You don't think he's... you know...'

She turned back to me with raised eyebrows.

'Well... become part of them?'

'What? No! You think Gío would still want to be his friend if Thibault had become a criminal?' She shook her wavy mane. 'Don't worry about that. Whatever brought him to you, it's not because he's running from the law.' Apparently, she found that very funny, because she burst out laughing. 'Can you imagine Beau in jail? Trying to charm all the female officers.' Her smile died, and she frowned. 'It might work at that. But don't worry!' she hastily added when my jaw dropped. 'He's fine. You're fine. You're both fine.'

All right, he was still on the straight and narrow. That didn't explain why he'd come to me, though.

'Has he ever said anything about... what Franck did?'

'You mean about why he's in jail?'

No. 'Well... yes. And no. I mean... he wouldn't come to me if he was... sort of... on Franck's side?' I hadn't thought of it before, but as soon as the thought popped into my head, my blood pressure spiked and I broke out in a cold sweat. They were family, after all. There could have been five years of resentment towards me building up in that house he supposedly escaped. He'd asked me for my side of the story and I'd made no attempt to smooth the matter over.

Maile fluttered her long lashes at me in obvious surprise. 'No! I mean, you're not the topic of weekly discussion, but he did mention he knew you when I told him I'd found work. From what I remember, he was more concerned about you than anything else. Certainly nothing negative. But that was two years ago, you know.'

I went back to work only slightly reassured and was still adjusting the lights outside when my client, a young woman named Kayleigh, arrived with her mother. After that I got too busy making them feel at home to worry about anything else. Kayleigh was excited, having received the shoot as a present for her twentieth birthday. There seemed to be a divide between clients who came to me through word of mouth and those who'd seen an ad somewhere. The women that'd heard about me from a recommendation needed more thinking time, but they had the most glorious transformations and were my most fervent advocates. Women who found me through an ad were more adventurous and often displayed far less nervousness. Kayleigh was an ad girl, ready to get going from the moment she walked in.

Beau stayed mostly out of the way, but couldn't help keeping an eye on his bike when we started shooting it. Kayleigh's cheeks turned a delightful shade of pink at the sight of him, which was perfect for my picture. As soon as we went back inside, though, he disappeared again. At quarter to four a double car horn blast from outside signified the arrival of Céline with cupcakes for *goûter*, the four o'clock snack I offered all my afternoon clients. They weren't a staple of the bakery, but she made them specially for me. She even brought them over, letting me know when to open the door for her as she usually entered with her hands full.

As I lowered the camera, Beau dashed in from upstairs. 'I'll get it.'

Kayleigh giggled when I made a face and sucked her bottom lip between her teeth at the sight of the colourful cupcakes. Click. That was a good one. Sometimes the best pictures are unplanned. We finished shooting an hour later, leaving the young woman and her mother exhilarated and satisfied. I promised them I'd have the photos by next week. Without fail, clients would ask me about that, even though I put my schedule in all the paperwork they'd had. Apparently there is an inherent insecurity, or perhaps an impatience, in finishing a shoot, that leaves people with no other option than to ask for reassurance on the subject. Or maybe it was my prices.

Thibault came down to help me clear away the cupcake wrappers and teacups once the two women had left. 'Anything else I can do?'

'No, thanks. Any luck finding another place to stay?'

He kept his head down. 'I still have a day.'

We went back to my house, passing through the courtyard. 'Right. I don't have any clients tomorrow, so I'll be editing and doing some admin in my office.' I always made sure to schedule days without shoots to do post-production and reveals. The moment people came back to view the photos and take them home was relatively short, but I liked to give them my full attention without time limits. Tomorrow, however, would not be filled with that positive energy. Just desk work. 'Since you won't have to do any heavy lifting, use your time wisely.'

He winked. 'Make myself indispensable. Check.'

'What are you, an old Irishman? Nobody winks any more, Thibault.'

'That's what you think. It's one of my best moves.' He winked again, making it almost impossible for me to keep a straight face.

'Well, it doesn't work on me. After tomorrow, I'm kicking you out. Now, do you like mushroom soup?'

'Who doesn't?'

He was an easy house guest, I had to give him that. I asked him about his drawings, and he showed me his sketchbook. No more of the dragons that used to fill it when he was seventeen, but the pretty girls remained. Many had something familiar about them, but I couldn't quite place it. When I asked about it, he shrugged, saying it was just his style. For the rest of dinner, we talked about things that had happened in the past years, but although I tried to steer the conversation in that direction, he kept silent about his reason for coming here. For old times I would let him stay, but this little mystery intrigued me.

He side-stepped my latest question with, 'I'm meeting Céline for a drink at the café—'

'Oh, you know her?' I shouldn't be surprised that he knew the prettiest girl in the village, but this was Céline we were talking about. She was... different? Not his type? Sensible. That's the one.

He stared at his phone, though the screen wasn't on. 'I... usually only see her when she comes to Villefranche. What I meant to ask was, want to come?'

I cringed. 'No, I don't think so. I still have a lot of work to do.' He didn't look surprised. In fact, he looked almost pleased. For some reason that irked me. Did he think he had me all figured out already? I'd show him! 'You know what, I will come. Let me get my purse.' Ha! I showed him.

And now I had to go out again.

Note to self: don't show Beau.

6

It makes her look like she jumped you

For lack of a more discreet friend nearby, Tiana stormed into Catherine's kitchen, pushing Banzaï out of the way. 'Look at this! I found this in my letterbox. It's utterly ridiculous.' She waved a white sheet of paper with only a few lines printed on it under Catherine's nose.

Catherine leaned back and took the offending paper. 'Tiana Lebrun, thou shalt not covet thy neighbour's gardener.' She burst into laughter that shook her plump little body. Wiping her eyes, she hiccoughed. 'Why not? He's very covetable.'

'It's not funny. Someone has made it look like I jumped him the moment I saw him. I've only even met him once. I think it's horrible for someone to stick their nose into my affairs like this, and then send me an anonymous letter about it. *Beurk!*'

The corners of Catherine's eyes crinkled when she peeked at the letter again. Before Tiana could stop her, she'd opened the door to the garden. 'Lucas! You're in print.'

Lucas's face appeared in the door frame, followed by the rest of him and the best part of a rake. Tiana could feel her cheeks heating when Catherine shoved the letter in his hands. His eyebrows shot up as he read. Then he flashed her a toothy grin.

'She said it makes her look like she jumped you.' Catherine's body still shook with silent laughter.

'You say that like I would have minded.'

Why did I come here? This was the worst idea ever. Could she still grab the letter and pretend it never happened?

'She thinks it's horrible.'

His face turned serious. 'Sending people unsigned letters is rather a nasty joke. Still, I think this message is less than harmful. I'm sorry it upset you, though. Are you all right?'

Tiana swallowed. Maybe the letter wasn't so bad if he didn't mind it. Now that he'd laughed about it, the whole thing didn't trouble her so much any more. Who knew his reaction had actually been her biggest worry?

She managed a small smile. 'I'm fine. Just wondering who would spend time on something dumb like this.'

He studied her face before answering. 'Don't give it another thought. Can I buy you a drink? I'm done for the day here, anyway. Right, Catherine?'

Catherine's eyes gleamed. 'You go right ahead and have a drink together. I'm sure you've loads to talk about.' She practically pushed them out of her kitchen. 'Oh, I've decided on what I want in that corner. I'm going for Brugmansia sanguinea and Berberis thunbergii.'

'Right. I'll be back when I've got those for you.'

Catherine closed the door behind them but gave Tiana a grinny wink and a wave through the little window when she looked back.

Lucas shoved his hands in his pockets, passing his truck on the way to the village centre. Cars coming back from work in the city blocked the bottleneck to the square, but the people inside smiled and waved at those already enjoying the late afternoon sun, chatting to their neighbours with a glass in hand. 'She knows what she wants, doesn't she?'

'She's never shy about broadcasting it, that's for sure.' She paused. 'I feel like I should apologise again, but I didn't write that letter.'

'Don't worry about it. Not on my account. Do you think they meant to hurt you, though?'

Tiana shrugged and paused outside her door. 'I can't imagine how. Or why. Hang on, I need to get my purse.'

Once inside, making sure Lucas couldn't see her, Tiana celebrated her nervousness by jumping up and down, shaking her curls and flexing her fingers. Five seconds of that, and she could handle the situation. She hadn't even had time to answer Lucas before Catherine had decided for her. Not that she minded, really. But five seconds of freaking out were needed to regain control. She transferred her wallet from her pocket to her purse, and stepped out. Now all she needed was something to talk about, but Lucas had that covered.

'I'm sorry to go on about this, but I'm trying to understand why someone would take the trouble to write you a letter that is so empty. It's not a threat. It's hardly an insult. Could it just be a joke?'

'Some joke. Catherine was the only one laughing. Come to think of it, she was the only one who knew that I'd met you. But she wouldn't do this. Besides, her reaction to it was genuine, I'm sure of it.'

'I'd say she also knows you well enough to come up with a better secret. I mean, if the point of this letter is to scare you – or warn you or even to insult you – they haven't put in too much effort. Even I could probably come up with a better insult than that. I mean, you write romance novels. All someone had to do was comment on how you do your research.'

My research! He was right, insulting someone came easily to him. Ugh, there went the cheeks again. Why could she never keep her feelings to herself?

'And scaring someone is even easier because you don't really need to get into any specifics. If you write an anonymous letter saying...' He had the decency to blush when he glanced her way. 'I'm so sorry, I didn't mean anything by that. It was stupid. I'm really sorry.'

'It's okay.' What else was she going to say? And it was kind of a cute apology.

They'd reached the café, found an empty table, and ordered their drinks.

'You're not French.' Oh good, that sounded like an accusation. Great way to start a conversation.

But Lucas laughed. 'You don't find my American accent charming? No, I came here five years ago...' He hesitated. 'Change of scenery. Was in the Navy before, but I prefer plants. How about you? Born and bred?'

Tiana nodded. 'I went to uni in Lyon, but more or less came running back. Too many people. I prefer them fictional.'

'And with happy endings, I presume. That doesn't happen often enough in real life.'

'No...' There was so much more to that remark, written all over his face, but even she knew that was not a getting-to-know-you subject. *Quick, find something else to say before the silence gets too awkward.* 'So what's your favourite plant?' *Lame – amend, immediately!* 'How does one become a gardener? Go to gardening school?'

'Ordinarily, yes. But in my case my dad was the school. He owns a small garden centre in Iowa. I think he's prouder of me now than when I went for a military career. Can't really blame him. I don't know what I was thinking.'

'Not your best decision?'

'Not by a long shot. Not my worst one either, but...'

'You're making me curious.'

He sipped his beer. 'Some other time. I don't think you want to tell me your worst decision, do you?'

Playing with the stem of her wine glass, she had to think about that. Her life had been relatively easy. Although she regretted doing things daily, none of them seemed the kind of Worst Decision of My Life Lucas was talking about. 'Mostly I regret telling Catherine anything.'

Lucas burst into a rolling laugh.

Surprised, Tiana continued, 'Honestly! Whenever I confide in her, which she tricks me into all the time, she makes fun of me for it.'

'Your life must be a roller coaster ride.'

'Don't you start.'

He stopped laughing but still wore a wide grin. 'If that's your biggest worry, then you are a walking advertisement for the quiet village life. You'd do well on the poster, too, with your pretty eyes.'

He called them pretty! Whoosh, went the cheeks. Tiana stared at her white wine, trying to suppress the biggest smile.

'You're easy to please, you know. Tell me, besides writing, what do you like to do?'

'Uhm... I, err...' Was there anything besides writing she liked to do? 'My friend Julie and I sometimes go out to eat or watch a movie.'

With that, the conversation turned to movies and pop culture in general, and Tiana finally relaxed a little, knowing she could talk about this forever. Lucas shared a love of superheroes, and they were so deep into their conversation that they hardly noticed when Julie, Thibault, and Céline joined them at their table.

7

Sometimes I'm on top, sometimes I'm in the gutter, sometimes both

I had one other friend in the village. After I'd decided to come back to Saint-Maurice, I'd looked her up and found she'd taken over the *bar-tabac*, a newsagent doubling as a café. Even in primary school, Jeanette Ta had been the one always throwing pretend tea parties and waiting on everyone. Now she'd made it her profession. When I'd been pacing at the other end of the square before coming in for the first time after coming back to the village, taking deep breaths and gathering courage, she'd come running out of the café, not only hugging me but immediately offering me drinks, food, and half the customers' friendships, whether they agreed or not.

Though still quite apprehensive, I was moved to tears by her generosity, but I soon found out I wasn't the only one she'd taken under her wing. The little establishment's walls were crammed full of paintings by a local artist. Jeanette held afternoon craft sales, talent shows, and networking events, and she invited speakers from all walks of life. None of those fitted the tiny bar room, of course, so most of it was done on the square. Officially, one needs a permit for those kinds of events, but when my mum is the mayor, you get away with stuff. Especially if you're the embodiment of a pillar of the community.

On a regular night like this one, though, Jeanette still didn't have to worry about filling her seats. The sun cast its last rays over the hilltop, illuminating only the very tip of the church tower. Without its warmth, the air would soon cool off, but everyone knew to bring a cardigan or a light jacket this time of year. And there was always wine to warm us up. Judging from the happy chatter, some people were already well beyond their first glass.

As we got closer to the tables dotting the plaza, I spotted Tiana at a table. With a man. A good-looking one at that. Talking and laughing. How interesting! We joined them at their table, which they didn't seem to mind. Good thing I showed Thibault after all. Now I had this new mystery to solve.

'Hiya! Who's this?'

'Lucas, this is Julie. Julie, Lucas, my neighbours' gardener.'

'Whom she should not covet, apparently.'

I raised my eyebrows, waiting for either the male model or the tomato to explain this curious remark.

'I only met Lucas this morning, and this afternoon I found a letter in my box that read, "Tiana Lebrun, thou shalt not covet thy neighbour's gardener". It's the most ridiculous thing I have ever received. And that includes some of my fan mail.'

'Oh! We must have a common enemy. I got a letter this morning, saying, "Julie Belmain, I know about your husband".'

'Really?' Tiana looked back and forth between me and Lucas. 'But... who?'

Lucas looked lost. 'What about your husband?'

Tiana waved a dismissive hand. 'She divorced him. He was an ass. But everybody knows that.'

'Exactly. It's just as empty a threat as yours. Not even a threat. I don't know what to call it. I showed it to Thibault and he thought it was a joke.' I turned to Beau, who only looked up when he heard his name.

'What? You think I'm a joke?'

'Pay attention if you want to be part of the conversation. I'm talking about the letter I got.'

That got Céline's attention. 'You got a letter too? I've heard loads of people have received one. Most of them talking about uncomfortable things in their lives, but nothing that would be of any use as blackmail. Some people think they're just someone's idea of a joke, but others think it's a little too much of a coincidence that the letters all came around La Mademoiselle's death. They think the two must be connected.'

Jeanette interrupted our conversation to take our orders, leaving me to contemplate Céline's words. Nothing ever happens here, and then two weird things at once? They had to be connected. I opened my mouth to say so, only to realise that to my left, Tiana and Lucas were talking about nerdy things, and to my right, Beau and Céline were talking about young people things. When Jeanette brought my wine, I toasted myself.

When the café was open, Jeanette was always too busy to talk. And the café was almost always open, it seemed. At moments like these I missed Franck. No, not Franck. Definitely not Franck. But someone like that. Someone who was just there. Someone to share everything with. I sighed. I picked the wrong someone.

Sipping my wine, I looked around the café seats spread out over part of the village square, the Place de l'Eglise. I knew almost all of the faces. I even remembered most of the names. It felt like home, and yet it didn't. I wasn't part of it any more, the way I'd been before I left. I was not as *libre* as I used to be here. A thought struck me that made me shiver. What if I ended up like La Mademoiselle? Not necessarily murdered, but alone. In the village, but not of the village. Shouting at people, 'Leave me be!' I'd have no one to blame but myself.

Actually, I could always blame Franck. That's what ex-husbands are for, right? And he was, as Tiana so delicately put it, an ass. Only, the fault still lay with me for not seeing that earlier. I considered the faces around me. That man with the balding patch, he used to be nice. Was he still? The woman in the flowery dress was a flirt. Now wearing a wedding ring. The party animal, the dreamer, the bore. Had I misjudged them all? Or had they changed? I knew I had.

I eyed my wine. I didn't know them. I wondered if they thought they knew me. The weirdo taking pictures of other people's bums. The divorcee coming back with her tail between her legs to the house her aunt left her in a village where her mother was the mayoress. And let's not forget that the Belmains had always been big shots in this village. My brother, the surgeon, still lived in La Grande Maison, the big house where my great uncle had died. For all the success in my chosen business, I was still the failure in my family.

'Julieee!'

'Bella.' Not noticing, or not caring about the lack of enthusiasm in my voice, the bottle blonde enclosed me in a weird, loose arm-hug. She would have been pretty if she didn't try so hard. But that was only the outside. Nice to your face, and then slide a knife in as soon as your back was turned. The get-it-off-your-chest-so-I-can-broadcast-to-the-entire-village-and-laugh-about-it variety.

'So good to see you! I think what you're doing is just absolutely ah-maze-ing. I wish I had the money to let you show my bum to the world. But then, I do a pretty good job of that myself, hahaaa!' That last syllable was in a tone so high, I expected all the dogs in the village to join in. When she pulled a chair away from another table to join ours, I suppressed a groan.

'Hiii, Lucas. Ooh, and who's this?' Lucas gave a polite smile, but Bella had already latched on to Thibault. While he brought out the dimples, I caught an eye-roll that Céline tried to hide. I really liked this girl.

'"This" is Thibault,' I mumbled.

'Call me Beau.'

'Oh, I *will*. As often as you'll let me.' She winked, he revelled, and I felt my stomach turn.

'How are you, Bella' I couldn't even make my voice pretend I really held an interest.

'Oh, you know me. Sometimes I'm on top, sometimes I'm in the gutter. Sometimes both.' She winked again and giggled, tossing her hair over her shoulder. 'Could really use a cigarette, though. You wouldn't have one, would you, *loulou*?'

Thibault shook his head and continued his conversation with Céline.

'Lucas?' She fluttered her eyelids when he didn't respond. 'Lulu?'

Another negative gesture. But apparently her need for nicotine was not great enough to ask any of the women. 'Nobody smokes around here any more. I had to quit because I was the only one outside all the time. It's all e-cigs and vaping. What's the point? Anywaaay... I was so sad to hear about Franck. How are you coping, huh?'

She made a comically sad face. One that could only inspire me to say, 'I'm fine.' How could the woman not notice I had no desire to speak with her?

'*Good!* Good. Well, you know you can *always* come to me if you need anything, don't you, *poupette*? Wouldn't want you to become the new Mademoiselle.' She giggled again, not even noticing my glare. How did she do that? How did she always know exactly where to put the finger?

'She must have had some friends, though. Someone found her, didn't they?' My tone was sharp but lost on Bella.

'Oh, yes, Madame Durand found her. Apparently she visited more often, but this time' – she leaned in – 'It was quite obvious that something was wrong. I heard Madame Durand came screaming out of the house, totally upset. She couldn't speak for half an hour! Apparently it was quite a gruesome sight. Poison, you know. Not even a murder with blood everywhere, but the place was still a mess. Her death must have been horrible.' Bella's eyes gleamed as she spoke. Not so horrible that she couldn't enjoy telling the story, apparently.

I remembered Laura Durand's state, which made even more sense if she hadn't found a normal dead body but a 'gruesome' one. Poor woman. 'Do they know why yet?'

'No! That's what everyone is talking about. There was no will and no relatives, so anything she owned now belongs to the state. And she never did anything interesting, so who would want her dead? All anyone can think of is that it's something to do with the letters, but how or why is a mystery.'

'Did you get one?'

'Hmmm. Something about me having had every man in the village. Like *that's* a secret.' Giggle. 'You know, I don't think they're going to solve this one. They never do. Twenty years from now, people will still be talking about these letters and the post-office lady, like they do now with the Woman in the Wine. Or Denis's wife.' She pursed her lips to one side. 'Hm, I should call him.'

How could she compare those two? Thirty years ago, a woman had died under suspicious circumstances, drowned in a wine vat. It was our local fodder for conspiracy theorists. But Denis had only been a widower for about six months. His wife, Coline, had died rather suddenly, though nobody but the likes of Bella suspected anything untoward. Unfortunately, those who did suspect had shouted loudly enough to land the grieving father of five in a police investigation.

'Don't. Coline died of natural causes. He has enough on his hands with those children, without you com—'

'Did she, though? That was the official version, but nobody really believes it.'

'They do, and so should you. It's because of people like you that he—'

'Ooh, Carlos! Carlos, *mon lapin*, I need— Excuse me, Julie, I've been wanting to talk to him. Buhbye, *poupette*.' She was up and out of sight before I could vent my built-up steam in her face, leaving me feeling about to blow. Did nobody even care that a woman had died? All they could talk about was the mystery of why!

'Juju...' Tiana's soft voice pierced the balloon inside of me, and I let out a long breath. 'It's only Bella.'

I smirked. 'She's just so...' I mimicked wringing her neck.

She wrinkled her nose. 'I know. She's... *beurk*. Everybody knows. We can add it to the pile of public secrets in the letters.'

'I don't even want to talk about them any more. They have nothing to do with me, and I'm going to let the police handle it all. Now, how's your new book coming along?'

We spent the rest of the evening chatting, and several glasses of wine later, I went home on Beau's arm, having forgotten all about any bad things or bad people in the world. When we passed the Durands' house, I looked up but couldn't help looking away after a second. Higher up the hill on the other side of the road, Tiana was having trouble saying goodbye to Lucas, who'd apparently walked her home. I smiled, yawned, and let Thibault pull me along.

8

We wouldn't ask you to investigate in any way

I was about to be crushed by a giant wine glass when the phone rang.

'Bwuhhh?'

'Sorry to call you so early, sweetie, but most people have already started their working day, you know.' My mother, who never gives an apology without a justification.

'Morning, *Maman*. What is it?'

'It's about Madame Braymand's death, of course. It's keeping me a little busy, as you can imagine.'

'Yes, I can. So why are you calling me?'

'I've been talking to Capitaine Gavel—'

'Oh, say hi from me.' Jacqueline Gavel had been an enormous help after she arrested Franck. We stayed in touch even after her transfer from fraud to personal violence.

'You can say hi yourself. Can you be at the *mairie* in twenty minutes? *À toute!*'

She'd hung up before I could mention my make-up alone took longer than twenty minutes on a good day, but Jacqueline Gavel had already seen me at my worst, so this would probably not be a good make-up day. I also had to settle for an old dress because it was easy to put on. I know it shouldn't matter, but it's the little things that make you grumpy sometimes.

Twenty-five minutes later I sat down at my mother's conference table in the village hall. 'Hall' is a big word for the building that housed the civil office, the library, and the village school, but it had no delusions of grandeur. The interior was simple and white, the only decorations being some stylised vines in the front office and a big painting from the 1980s that showed the *vendanges*, the picking of grapes at the end of summer, that hung in the conference room where I now sat.

My mother presided, looking every bit the stylish *Française*, except for the hand-crocheted accessories. She used the finest threads and made almost lace-like pieces, but I supposed it was clear to see where I got my lack of regard for current fashion. She was efficient and business-minded in almost everything she did, except for a love of books, fine crochet work, and everything Disney.

Jacqueline was seated across from me with her colleague. Her short, dark brown hair was beginning to grey, and her sizeable nose gave her face a sharp edge. When talking to anyone but criminals, however, she almost always smiled, the little wrinkles around her eyes taking the edge off again. The dark blond man in his mid-thirties with her did not seem as pleased to see me. His eyebrows hung low over his eyes and his arms were crossed.

'Looking good, Jacquie.'

'Good morning, Madame Belmain,' she replied with a wink her colleague couldn't see. 'This is Brigadier-chef Marc Froment.' She paused as we acknowledged each other with a nod. 'As *Madame le Maire* has already informed you, we're investigating the death of Madame Braymand. Unfortunately' – she exchanged a quick look with her partner – 'people are extremely reluctant to talk to us. Even more than we're used to. Now, my colleague disagrees with this' – another quick glance, while Froment shook his head, mostly to himself, it seemed – 'but the mayor has suggested we invite you to... help us out. You live here, you know the people. You walk around with your camera and talk to them, but you have no official capacity that could scare them off, as it would with your mo— the mayor.'

Froment crossed his arms while I tried to work out exactly what it was they wanted me to do. 'If you think they see me as one of them...' I gave my head a little shake. 'They talk to me, sure, but it's never more than a casual conversation.'

'Madame Belmain, this is a small village where a big event has taken place. Even if the victim was not a big name, murder itself is significant enough to have everyone talk about it. I'm sure you've already experienced this.'

It was a statement, but her eyes questioned me, so I tried to shrug as neutrally as I could.

'Naturally, we wouldn't ask you to investigate in any way. There are no questions we would like you to ask. But when you do speak to people about the murder, keep your ears open for anything that might help us in *our* investigation. You are bound to pick up more clues from casual conversation than people are willing to give us in an interview.'

Talk to everyone in the village. This had my mum written all over it. Did she not realise I had a business to run? Joining the community and all of its judgement was not a priority right now. Of course I wanted justice for Madame Braymand, and okay, I was dying to know who would kill a relatively harmless recluse and why, but I had no intention of getting caught up in this investigation.

Already the silence was becoming awkward, but I had my conversation with Bella the previous night in mind. 'People may have already made their mind up about what happened.'

Jacqueline nodded. 'That's exactly the kind of thing we're looking for. Even if people are wrong in their accusations, one person will point to another, who will point to another, and by the tenth, we'll have picked up a lead that will take us to the actual perpetrator.'

'Won't I just be wasting your time with false leads?'

'Yes,' Froment grumbled.

'No.' She didn't look at him, but her lips stiffened. 'Right now we have no leads at all. Of course, that's not entirely true, but apart from the woman who found the body, nobody seems to have been in contact with the deceased. Someone must have been, though.'

'Because it wasn't a burglar? Oh right, no blood.' Bella had called it messy. At the time I'd been too annoyed, but now I wondered what she meant.

Jacqueline and Froment did some heavy looking back and forth. 'Who told you that?'

'Bella. Dudevant. Who else?' I added with a smirk to my mother.

'We did talk to her.' Jacqueline nodded again, while Froment was trying to hide a grin. 'Gave us a lot of information, but nothing useful. How did she know this? Did she say?'

I thought back to the night before. 'I don't think so. She said it was messy, that's all.'

'That it was.' She caught my gaze. 'This demonstrates you will indeed be able to find out more than we will. You see that, don't you?'

I winced. If I said no now, it would look like I was hindering the investigation by not cooperating. 'You know, people might be more willing to talk to me if I have a nice bit of new information. How was she killed?' Hey, I should be able to get something out of this.

Jacqueline leaned back in her chair. Froment shook his head with determination. Ah well, I tried.

I sighed. 'All right, if you think it'll help. But don't get your hopes up. I moved away from Saint-Maurice, so now I'm just as much an outsider as you are.'

'I'm sure that's not true. Thank you, Julie.' *Maman* stood up. Apparently, the meeting was over. 'And thank *you* too. Your job is difficult enough. I'm glad we can be of assistance.' They shook hands as I rose slowly.

'One more thing...'

Froment narrowed his eyes. 'Yes?'

'I have an assistant. Is it okay if I get him involved in this?'

My mother's eyebrows shot up. Froment opened his mouth, but Jacqueline cut in, 'Fine. As long as they're discreet.'

We all said our goodbyes, my mother insisting she would call me soon, but Jacqueline stopped me outside. She waited until Froment had closed the car door, then turned to me with a twinkle in her eye.

'So what's this about a new male assistant? I didn't know you needed help.'

'Ugh, and I don't.'

'Reeeally?'

Boy, did she have it wrong. 'Relax, it's just someone who needed a place to stay.'

'So do I know him?'

'Maybe. Do you remember Beau?'

Her jaw dropped. 'You can't mean Thibault Fouquet. You and Beau??'

'No, not me and Beau! Ew, we used to be related. What is wrong with you?'

'Okay, well, you know... Beau... kind of has this reputation.'

Froment rapped on the car window, tapping his watch. Jacqueline took a step towards the car, but I held her arm.

'What reputation? Nothing illegal, right?' That would mean a serious misjudgement on my part, but I wanted to be sure.

Jacqueline snorted. 'No, nothing illegal. Let's just say he's a... Well... loose morals or something? I've got to go, Julie. I'll call you later. Thanks for doing this.' And she was gone.

Great. Not only had I been enlisted to talk to people who didn't really seem to like me, but my now-almost-official-but-still-under-protest assistant was a notorious Casanova. My heels clicked on the pavement as I went to my car. Normally I'd walk, but *Maman* had only given me twenty minutes to get there. I'd better redo my make-up when I got home.

'Thibault!' I admit, it was a less than ladylike approach to be standing at the bottom of the stairs bellowing up, but I was getting seriously grumpy. Not even the naked chest appearing at the top of the stairs could cheer me up. Beau was buttoning up his jeans, unruly blond mop hanging over sleepy eyes.

I pointed at him with my mother-finger. 'Absolutely no sleeping with any of my clients!'

'Wha? What time is it?' He put the heel of his hand to his eye.

'Just after ten. You heard me.'

'Who have you been talking to?' he mumbled, but then apparently woke up enough to switch the dimples on. 'Not even before they're your clients? Might do your business some good.'

'No! No sleeping with anyone who is now, or ever was, or could maybe possibly at some point in the future become my client!' I grumbled a little. Like I needed his kind of boost. My business was doing just fine, thank you very much. No males required.

But as for this talking with people business... Don't get me wrong – I really don't hate people. I also love to talk. I talk all the time. To friends, to clients, to the person next to me in the plane who wishes I would shut up already. But in this village, you're very much either one of them, or not one of them. I used to be one of them. I had grown up here, after all. But I moved away to marry, only to divorce in a few years. And although I'd come back a successful photographer, the defeat of divorce was more important to them. And now I had this live-in... Ugh.

I slammed the door to my office but couldn't concentrate on the photos I'd taken yesterday. Maybe I should take my camera and start on the talking. Then if it didn't work, I had at least tried. I swivelled my chair, but what do you know, my camera was asleep. Can't wake a sleeping camera, everyone knows that. I sighed, feeling like the coward I was.

Still procrastinating, I ambled up to the front window to open the blind and let in some sunshine. Tiana came walking up my driveway, followed by Lucas. I smiled. With all her romance writing, Tiana had not had the best of luck in love. This one, however, seemed a much better bet.

'Hey you!' She kissed my cheek. 'Been out?'

'Not really. Just a visit to the *mairie*, which was kind of frustrating. I was going to go through some of my new photos, but you are as good a distraction as any. Come on in.'

Tiana had automatically veered towards my studio. She knew that's where I kept my cookies. If I keep them in the house, I know I'll eat them all in one sitting. Some days I'll still do that, even with the cookies in the studio, but at least I'll have burnt two calories coming over and going back. Plus, of course, all the calories I burn baking new cookies, but that doesn't change with where I keep them. That's just how I kid myself that it's okay eating all those cookies.

Lucas, being new here, tried very hard to keep his eyes on the white parts of my studio, the walls and the furniture. The brightly coloured photos on the walls flaunted the plump 'be-ooty' of my clients. I came up with that word myself. Still wondering where to use it, though.

Lucas cleared his throat. 'I wouldn't have thought pin-ups would go over well in the French countryside.'

'Ah, and that is why I make a lot of money. French women like their ooh-la-la too, you know.' I winked, he blushed, I giggled, Tiana glared, and then I blushed. Hey, I flirt. It's... er... branding. I gave Tiana an apologetic look and tried a different approach. 'You're American, so should we be calling you Loocas?'

'It's actually my middle name. My parents call me Burke.'

Tiana wrinkled her nose. *Beurk?*

'That's why I went with Lucas.' He laughed at her disgusted expression.

Aww, how cute. All googly-eyed, they sat down on the sofa together.

I made coffee and joined them. 'Have a cookie.' I opened the tin to find only two cookies left. 'Oh. Thibault must have found them.'

On cue, the door to the stairwell opened, letting in a clothed and styled Beau.

'Did you eat my cookies?'

'What cookies? Hi, Tiana, Lucas.'

I smoothed my skirt over my hips. Liar. I turned back to Tiana. 'So, anything new?'

'Not since last night.' Tiana took one of the cookies and handed Lucas the other. Drat. 'You?'

'Actually, that's why I went to the *mairie*. They want me to help out with the murder investigation.'

Tiana looked puzzled.

Lucas shifted in his seat. 'Are you good with that sort of thing?'

'She's not. Why would they ask you? That's quite unusual, isn't it?' Beau came out of the kitchen munching on a piece of the baguette I'd brought home from the village.

'Oh, thanks for the vote of confidence.' Cookie thief. 'I'm not actually helping them, though. They just want me to tell them if I hear anything out of the ordinary. But that means they expect me to talk to people.'

Beau swallowed, pointing at me with the stick of bread. 'You'll need an assistant. I bet I could make them talk. We'll have that killer in no time.'

'Maybe you should join the police, then. Make your mother proud.'

He waved the bread around. 'You can mock all you want, but take Tiana here. You don't suspect her because she's your friend.' He stepped towards her and got in her face. 'But where were *you* when the murder took place?' He straightened and turned back to me, leaving Tiana with wide eyes and an unsure smile. 'When *did* the murder take place?'

Heh. This might actually be fun. 'You're absolutely right.' I put on a grave voice. 'Tiana, where *were* you on... Oh, I don't know when it was either. Hang on.' I shot off a text to Jacqueline. Time of death probably wasn't secret, right?

While I was typing, Thibault struck up a conversation.

'Five years,' Lucas answered him. 'I thought I'd go back to Naples after I got out of the Navy because I was stationed there for a while, but when I went back, it had lost its attraction. So after a bit of roaming, trying stuff here and there, I ended up in Saint-Maurice.'

'And stayed.'

'Obviously. I answered an ad from the school saying they needed help with sports classes. I still do that every Wednesday, but people were so friendly that I thought I might try opening a business. It worked. So well, in fact, that I'll have to hire my own help soon.'

Tiana smiled at him. Look at her, already feeling proud. How long had she known him, exactly? My phone pinged.

'Tuesday night! Where were you Tuesday night, Ti?'

'At home, writing.'

'Can anyone verify that?' Thibault looked at Lucas. He'd obviously missed the part where she met him only yesterday morning.

My phone pinged again. 'Oh! So apparently La Mademoiselle was killed with a plant-based poison, probably a mixture of datura and something called colchicum. It—'

'Naked ladies.'

Everyone stared.

'Uhm, Lucas, I realise my studio can be a bit distracting to a man, but—'

He shook his head. 'No, no. It's a plant. Autumn crocus, also called naked ladies, because the flowers grow before the leaves. Quite poisonous, especially the seeds. Combined with datura, I'm afraid that was... not a pleasant death. As far as there is such a thing.'

Not pleasant. The words made me curious, but with Bella calling the death a mess, I decided to give this particular bit of info a miss. I wasn't getting any more involved than I had to.

Tiana touched her hand to her throat. 'Who would do such a thing to La Mademoiselle? She was harmless.'

'That's what we're supposed to find out, isn't it?' Beau asked.

'We're not supposed to do anything of the sort. All they asked me to do is to listen to other people talk. No investigating required!' I gave him a stern look, but he shrugged it off. 'I wonder who would know about these poisons, though.' I wiggled my phone. 'There's the usual amount of probablies and likelies here, but the poison was brushed onto the glue of her envelopes. She must have licked so many that she ingested enough of it to k—' Oh. Should I have shared that with everyone? See, this is why they shouldn't have got me involved! I tried to control the damage with, 'Probably best not to spread this information around—'

But Beau had already moved on. 'So she was the one sending all those letters!' His eyes twinkled in triumph.

'Well, no, that doesn't work,' I said, thinking back. 'Mine came in a self-adhesive envelope. Yours?'

Tiana bit her lip, then nodded.

'Did you get one, Lucas?'

'A self-adhesive envelope with the threat of revealing a public secret? No. But then I don't have public secrets.'

'Just private ones, huh.' I winked and Tiana glared again. Oops.

Letting out a nervous cough, he tapped a beat on the armrest. 'Don't think I had anything to do with this, though, just because I know the plants. If there are instructions for building a bomb online, I'm sure you can find this too.'

Tiana gave a shy smile. 'Nobody suspects you.'

'Except me!' Beau put up his hand. 'I suspect everyone from now on. Even Julie. But not myself, obviously. I know I didn't do it.'

'I didn't either!'

'Nor me.'

'I already told you I didn't do it.'

I stood up to make some more coffee. 'That settles it then, none of us did it. Deal with it, Thibault.'

Beau huffed. 'She may have died on Tuesday night, but if it was from poison on envelopes, that stuff could have been there for ages. Anyone could have done it at any time, so you're all still suspects to me.'

As I scooped coffee grounds into the *cafetière*, I thought about that. As much as Beau was enjoying his exaggeration, he was right. In effect, the poison could have been planted years ago. The person who had it in for La Mademoiselle might even have moved away from the village by now.

Thibault strolled into the kitchen and picked up two of the coffees. 'So who are we talking to first?'

'*We* are not talking to anyone. *You* are going to call your friends and find another place to stay. Tonight is your last night.'

'Last night for what?' Tiana asked as she took a mug from me.

I motioned my head towards Thibault, who ignored the whole thing.

'You already went next door without me. I bet I could have helped.' He struck a pose to underline exactly why I was right not to take him along.

Tiana grinned. 'I doubt she'd be susceptible to your charm, Beau. She's pretty devoted to her husband, though he seems an odd fish to me. Some couples are like that. A woman in my knitting group in Villefranche is the same. Doting on a husband that's super tight on the money. She saved up for a pair of boots, but then had to hide them with a friend so the husband wouldn't find out.'

My exclamation of 'Hide boots??' drowned out Lucas's 'You're in a knitting group?', but the amusement in his pulled-up eyebrows caused Tiana to blush.

'Devoted or not, she's very upset. I don't think you could have helped, Thibault.'

Beau huffed. 'I still think you should have let me come. You know I'm good with nervous women.'

Lucas snorted into his coffee.

'You know how I learned this? When we're out and I get a bit of... you know... interest, I always go for the one in worst need of a good time.'

I made a face. 'How noble.'

'Also, unlike most guys, I'm actually good with crying women. Because mostly they just want to get something off their chest. And once they start talking, you'll find out if there is anything you can do. And sometimes they really just want to get hot and—'

'Stop! Please! All right, *I'm* going to get my camera and do my civic duty. *You* are out of here.'

Here's the good thing about best friends: you can throw them out before they've finished their coffee. Here's the good thing about Tiana: she will keep her giggles to herself until she's out of earshot. But once we were outside, she burst out laughing. 'That's hilarious! Juju, you should keep him, if only for entertainment value.'

I groaned. He had better find somewhere else to stay, or we might end up with two murders in the village.

9

I'm going to fight the Darkness

I had three names on my list of people to try and talk to. Laura Durand had mentioned the Dutch lady, Marie Madora; Mylène Grasset, the school teacher; and number one citizen Apolline Bailly. My first port of call was Marie, since she scared me the least. Also, she would probably be home this time of day.

Her house was on the east side of the village, whereas mine was on the west side. As I wandered around the houses between my own and that of the Madora family, I hesitated at several, trying to work out if the same people lived there as before I left. The yellow stone provided a warm backdrop for the well-watered gardens, but most windows had either shutters or curtains closed to keep the sun, and my curious eyes, out. Warm outside, cold inside. Like the people living there. One of them had been cold enough to take another person's life. More warmth gone. Although Madame Braymand had already turned pretty cold during her life.

I passed another walled garden. Keeping them in, keeping me out. I knew these streets so well. They were so familiar, and yet strange. Like a dream version of a distorted memory. A nightmare actually, where anything might happen at any time, but not in a good way. This village was supposed to make me feel at home and at ease, but now I might talk to a murderer after every corner I turned.

I'd reached Marie Madora's house. While most houses around here were the standard oblong with a gently sloping roof, hers only had that at its heart. Over the years the various owners had built annexes, extensions, and other pustules onto it, until it had become the hodgepodge of living quarters it was today. Hidden under climbing plants and behind richly bejewelled fruit trees, though, the house exuded a certain messy charm, mirrored by a garden strewn with toys, bikes, and gardening tools. Little purple flowers in a well-kept bed seemed to smile at me in the sunlight. Their shiny cupped petals and slender white stems contrasted with the dark earth they emerged from much more vividly than the bushes around them. 'Take our picture,' they screamed. I obliged.

'Gorgeous, aren't they?' Marie Madora emerged from around the house, a frilly apron covering a sparkly lilac dress. She always wore no more than half-length sleeves, since she was born with the lower half of her left arm missing. 'I love having flowers in the garden at this time of year, when most of the other plants have given up on blooming. They lift the spirit so.'

Marie had learnt the language from books, and it showed. Even after living here for over ten years, she mispronounced words, mixed up idioms, and confessed to translating Dutch expressions if she felt like they should fit.

'They're lovely,' I admitted. Now how was I going to bring up the murder? I should have thought this through. My camera had given me a reason for my presence but no words to bring up my actual reason for being there.

She looked at me expectantly, but when nothing came filled the silence with, 'How is your business? Your new studio is the little nose of the salmon, I heard.'

'Yes, it turned out just the way I wanted it to.' I assume that's what she meant. 'But I'm glad to finally be rid of the dust and the builders.'

She nodded her black bob. 'Mmm, I know what you mean. Our house is beautiful now, but we spent almost a year camping out in our own home.'

Another silence. Apparently, all social skills leave me if I have alternative motives. 'You should come by my studio and have a look at it.' Ha! A stroke of genius, if I may say so myself. If I couldn't think of anything to say now, maybe I'd have better luck on familiar turf.

'Oh, that's sweet, thank you!'

She said it with conviction, but her whole attitude told me she wouldn't come. Bye-bye stroke of genius. I had to think of something to say quickly now or she'd be off, and I'd be standing there in her garden with nothing left to do but photograph flowers. Not my thing. Wrong curves.

'How are the boys?' Ugh. If this was what my social skills had become, I might as well quit now.

Marie Madora smiled politely, as though she knew my interest couldn't possibly be genuine. 'Oh, they are my pride and joy. But they do take up almost all of my time. In fact, I'd better get back to them. Feel free to take as many pictures as you like of the garden.'

No, no, no! Don't leave! I was about to ask her the name of the flowers, just to keep her here, when she froze in her turn with a curious expression.

'Ciao.'

I turned to see Beau coming down the street and almost groaned. Just what I needed, my blond Don Juan.

'You were gone so long, I thought you might need some help. But you were right, she would be a great model. Hi, I'm Thibault.'

I blinked a few times while Marie introduced herself. She was probably quite pretty, but you couldn't tell underneath that mask of make-up. Although the mask itself was quite pleasant to look at, Marie had literally put on a face. Pity it was someone else's.

So why had Beau made up that ridiculous lie? Someone hiding behind that much make-up is not interested in showing her derrière to the world. But the smile she gave him was much more than polite.

'Model for what? Julie didn't mention it. I've never known you to be shy, Julie. If you want something, just ask me. Come in, come in!'

And just like that, Beau had done it. For a moment, I didn't know whether to feel grateful or annoyed. Annoyance took over, but only at myself when I realised I'd been touched by the green monster. Making sure no one was looking, I plucked the jealousy out of my head and deposited it by the door. As I stepped inside, I stuck my tongue out at it.

A giant penguin judged me from a poster on the wall. I looked round to see more and more penguins displayed on every surface in the living room. Penguins on slides, penguins in fights, penguins in old-fashioned leather pilot helmets with goggles. I supposed a penguin collection wasn't any stranger than a key collection. Although keys, of course, unlock things that would otherwise have stayed mysterious. Was there a bit of method in this penguin madness as well?

A cute boy of about seven years old meandered into the room, singing 'Frère Jacques' but in woofs, as if he were a dog. He peered at us with a mixture of curiosity and mischievousness then disappeared again, never breaking off his song.

'So, penguins, huh?' Thibault stated.

Marie chuckled. 'Yes, it got a bit out of hand. When we sold the business, we joked to our family we needed to move away. Maybe to Antarctica. They've been giving us penguin-related stuff every time they visit. Have a seat. Would you like some coffee?'

Since I'd abandoned my second cup to come here, I accepted, and Marie disappeared to where I assumed the kitchen was. Inside, the house was modern and neat but again strewn with toys, colouring pencils, and video games controllers.

When she came back into the room, Thibault was studying a bunch of penguins on swings and see-saws. 'These are funny. But why Antarctica? It's not really the most obvious choice, even for northerners such as yourself.'

Marie's smiled but avoided his gaze when she handed him his coffee. 'It was just a silly joke. We needed a break from inflatable water slides, and Antarctica seemed to be about as far away from them as we could get. France wasn't that, but we thought it would be a better place to raise the kids we wanted.'

Beau nodded. 'Better climate.' He shivered and rubbed his arms to underline his point.

Marie set down my coffee on the table and took a chair opposite me. 'Yes. More children too. But we ended up surrounded by penguins after all. Of course, I could get rid of them, but I've grown attached to them. Maybe one day we'll visit the real things.'

'Antarctica sounds just about as unusual as inflatable water slides.' I took a sip of coffee and held the cup in front of me as a kind of shield. It might be innocent small talk, but it still felt like some form of betrayal. I would have said exactly the same things if I came by as a friendly neighbour, but now that I was supposed to talk to her to find out more about her, I felt like a spy. But not in the exciting way. Insincere, somehow.

Marie laughed. 'You're one to talk about unusual! We sold the business to spend more time with the boys. How did you even come up with your idea?'

I shrugged. 'Oh, you know... No one else was doing it.'

Beau snorted as he put back a large penguin actually wearing a tuxedo. 'She's been the butt of the family's jokes ever since.'

I raised an eyebrow. This was news to me. I wondered if it was true, or whether Beau thought he was being funny.

Marie laughed her tinkly laugh again. 'Seems like it was a gap in the market. A sensible business move, though. I've heard several people rave about your pictures.'

'Really?' Sunshine broke through the clouds of my apprehension. She wouldn't make that up, would she?

'Absolutely! So tell me, why would you want me to model for you, if your business is doing so well?'

I felt my palms getting sweaty, while I shot Beau a look. He'd better help me out with this ridiculous lie. But no, he was bent over a group of penguins on roller-skates with his back to me, his shoulders shaking with silent laughter. He was so out of my house after tonight!

'Well...' Work, brain! 'I, err...'

'Mummy! I'm going to fight the Darkness!' The little boy's voice came from another room, and Marie answered him between sips of coffee.

'That's nice, dear. Will you be done in time for *déjeuner*? I'm sorry, Julie, you were saying?'

For a moment, I'd hoped she'd forget the question, but no such luck. 'It was actually...' Ah! Here we go! 'Because of the murder.'

She looked puzzled. And slightly alarmed. 'The... murder?'

'Yes, it was a bit of a haphazard remark. I was worried that the murder would scare away my clientèle, and I'd need to find some models for advertising purposes. That's why I mentioned you.'

'Oh, I see!' Marie leaned back with a relieved smile. 'That's very flattering, thank you.'

'So far, though, I think we'll be all right. I've not had any cancellations yet.' For some reason, I expected her to be devastated about losing her chance at a free shoot, but she didn't seem too bothered by it. Hm.

'Terrible thing, though, isn't it?' Beau finally sat down on the couch beside me. I braced myself for the third degree. 'Everyone's talking about it.'

Marie checked her nails, cleaning under one with another. 'Are they?'

'Yes, because of the letters.'

Marie's fingers stilled, and her voice was on the high side when she asked, 'What letters?'

Beau steamed ahead quite casually. I had to hand it to him, he seemed to actually be good at this. 'Oh, I thought everyone in the village had had one. Julie's letter said something about her husband.'

Marie now fixed her eyes on me. 'Oh.' A slight pause. 'Really?'

'You haven't had one?' Beau asked just as casually.

The small but sharp intake of breath would have gone unnoticed if I weren't paying attention. But it confirmed to me that when she said 'no', it was an absolute lie.

'No! Strange, really, isn't it? In France, everything is still done by post. When are they going to join the twenty-first century?'

'Makes you wonder why they closed the post office,' I ventured.

She shrugged with a half-smile. Maybe I should lay it on a little more thickly. 'My condolences, by the way – I heard you and Madame Braymand used to be quite good friends.'

She huffed. 'Well, yes, years ago. When we'd just arrived, we didn't know anyone, and I had some trouble getting used to a new place. Claire, of course, knew everyone and everything that was going on in the village. She took me under her wing and introduced me to most of my current friends. There were a bunch of us getting together regularly: Claire and me with Mylène Grasset and Apolline Bailly. And sometimes your mother. But after she lost her job, Claire descended into bitterness faster than any one of us could pull her up and out. The last few years, I don't think she was in contact with any of the old group. Other than Madame Whatsername, Durand, and the estate agent, no one ever seemed to visit.'

'Monsieur Tariel visited La Mademoiselle?' Another import Saint-Maurician. Laurent Tariel had a Latin-American accent, called everyone by the diminutive of their name, and was grossly out of place in a rural French village.

Marie made a face. 'Visited is hardly the right word. He came by to pester her into selling. Such a creepy character.' She shivered. 'Oh, hello, *schat*.'

A tall, black man with a thin moustache entered through the garden doors, mumbling greetings. Maarten Madora always made a bit of a surly impression at first, but if you looked closely, you saw the lights of humour dancing in his eyes. I'd met him once before, during the *nuits de rosé*, where he'd looked quite uncomfortable until he cracked a joke that made everyone laugh. He'd still looked uncomfortable, so I decided to talk to him to make him feel more welcome. That's when I'd discovered those lights.

Marie sought her husband's support. 'Don't you think Tariel is a slick Janus?'

Pursing his lips, Maarten shrugged. 'I think it's an act. But I seem to be the only one.'

The conversation took a turn, and I couldn't steer it back again. After five minutes of trying I gave up, and that's when another of her boys, this one about eleven, came in.

'Mum, I can't find my... Oh, hey, you're the butt lady, aren't you?'

From the corner of my eye, I could see Thibault breaking into a cold sweat trying not to burst out laughing. Marie turned pink and quickly reprimanded her son with an apologetic glance to me.

'But Mum! Everyone at school calls her that.'

'Then everyone in school should wash their mouth with soap.'

I felt I should say something to defend myself. 'I don't really mind if they call me that, but it'd have to be for the right reason. Do you know why they call me butt lady?'

'You take pictures of people's butts, don't you?' He took great pride in pronouncing the word 'butt' as loudly as he dared.

'That's right. And do you know why?'

He shrugged.

'Because all butts are beautiful.'

'Heh heh, butts.' He grinned and ran off.

Marie put her hand on my knee. 'It was a valiant effort. There's only so much you can do with an eleven-year-old boy's mind.'

Not much later, Beau and I said our goodbyes, repeating our invitation to drop by the studio.

'Do you think she did it?' Beau asked when we were at a safe distance.

'I don't know.' I sighed. 'How would I know? Fortunately, I only have to talk to them. They only asked me to be on the look-out for suspicious statements, and I have heard none.'

Except maybe that I still wasn't sure why they'd moved countries after selling the business. Marie had said both that they wanted children, and that they wanted to spend more time with the children, but I dismissed the discrepancy as unimportant.

'Maybe it was the husband,' Thibault mused. 'It's always the silent ones.'

'And you know this... how?'

'Because I'm not one, and I know my type.' Beau ignored me, and went off on a rave about his type, and why it must have been Maarten Madora who killed Claire Braymand. Never mind motive.

But who else was there? Mylène Grasset taught at the village school, but she'd moved to Villefranche years ago, and never came to the village outside of school hours any more. Apolline Bailly was the wife of one of the village council members. He was the CEO of some company or other. All very respectable and quite posh. And then there was my mother. It couldn't be her.

Could it?

No!

I sighed again. Not my job. I only needed to talk. To possible murderers. But then, I couldn't let this scare me into leaving and never trusting anyone again. Take Marie, for instance. Even if she was a killer, she must have had a reason? Sometimes good people get pushed into doing bad things. That's what Jacqueline had told me after Franck went to jail and I was ready to give up on humanity. It didn't hold up for Franck, of course, but it had given me a little more faith in the rest of the world. Time to boost my own faith and do what my friend had asked me.

Fate found this the opportune moment to drop in one of my least likely suspects. A silver Mercedes stopped at the side of the road and out came *maitresse* Mylène. No, that's not strong enough. She emerged, materialised as if she'd been on Mount Olympus a second before. This effortlessly elegant child-rearing goddess, the image of graceful French fashion, with a dazzling smile and a store of patience the size of Provence. If ever I were to have children, I would want them in her care.

I admit I was a little starstruck. Or maybe a lot. Over someone who wasn't even a real star. But if you'd seen her, you'd know what I mean. Her hair ranged from almost blonde in summer to dark copper in winter, but at the moment it was somewhere in between. The whole picture just... worked. She was the epitome of class. Apart from an introduction for Beau, all I could utter was a compliment on her blouse, a bright white number with a wide collar that showed off her bronze skin.

She accepted it with one of her blinding smiles, one that strangely seemed to have no effect on Thibault, who asked, 'Do they really call her the butt lady?'

Mortified. That's what I was.

Mylène Grasset blinked her long black lashes a few times, then sighed delicately. 'We do try to teach the children that that is not a nice thing to say, but unfortunately, yes, they do say it sometimes.'

He pointed at me with his thumb. 'She says she's proud of it because all butts are beautiful.'

'Oh!' Tiny smile wrinkles made her even more radiant. 'How marvellous. I shall have to incorporate that into my teaching.'

'How are the children coping with a murder in the village?' I knew I was being blunt, but I probably wouldn't have another opportunity to speak to her.

Mylène touched her fingers to her throat. 'I... Well... fortunately, they're children. Some find it exciting, some find it sad, but most don't seem to be too upset about it.'

'How about you?' Thibault asked. 'Weren't you friends?'

A rare spark of anger flashed in Mylène's eyes. 'That was long ago, before she started yelling at the children. Now, if you'll excuse me, Marcus left his *doudou* at school, and I know he won't be able to sleep without it.' She held up a raggedy stuffed rabbit as if it was part of the crown jewels, and we stepped aside to make way for her majesty.

'Pretty,' Thibault said when she was out of earshot.

I couldn't even begin to describe how much of an understatement that was, so I didn't answer. Something else occupied my mind. Though I honestly didn't really mind being the butt lady, it did bother me that it was not meant as a compliment. So would it have been just one parent letting that slip in front of their child, or was that the way everyone saw me? The only way to find out was to – gulp – talk to them.

'So she's one of the suspects?' Even Beau now looked unsure.

'You're the one suspecting everyone. But I regret to say I'm not done talking just yet.'

Now what excuse could I possibly have to talk to an estate agent?

10

This is it! Do not pull back!

Tiana fidgeted with her nails. Why had she agreed to spend today with Lucas? A whole day was a very long time to spend with someone you'd only met the previous day. Surely they would run out of things to say soon? The visit to Julie had led to a fun conversation about true crime shows and how she couldn't stop watching them, even though they made her question the sensibility of living alone on a relatively isolated road just outside the village, with only some elderly neighbours.

She'd liked that he said he'd protect her. The shameless flirt. He had her constantly blushing. If she were one of the heroines of her novels, she'd say something sassy. It struck her in that case she should be able to come up with something. At his next joke, she opened her mouth and racked her brain, but all she accomplished was that his face turned more and more amused at the deepening glow on her cheeks. In the end she cast down her eyes, expecting more teasing, but he let it go with no more than a big grin.

They'd come to the first houses of the village. The autumn sun bounced off the yellow stones, a reminder of the friendliness of the people living there. Shutters and curtains kept the sun out, but the doors were always open for friends and neighbours. Living here was like wrapping yourself in a warm blanket, comforting and familiar.

'How about lunch at the café?' Lucas asked.

Had he still not had enough of her? 'Sure. The owner's a friend of mine. She always gives me and Julie our soup for free. But then we always leave a tip that more than covers the soup.' She shrugged. 'Goes without saying. It's our thing, I suppose.'

Lucas smiled in answer. They now passed the *mairie* on the Place de l'Eglise. Jeanette Ta ran the café at the corner of the Rue de Cézanne.

'So how come I've never seen you before in the five years I've lived here? I know most of the other people around here.'

Tiana bit her lower lip. 'Then you're obviously a more social person than I am.' It wasn't that she didn't like her neighbours. But when imaginary and digital friends are so much more entertaining, who needs real people? Except maybe a gorgeous gardener who hadn't realised yet that she was not as interesting as he thought... 'I do know most of the people here. I just spend a lot of my time typing. And I suppose I'm not exciting enough for people to drop me casually into the conversation.'

Lucas pulled a chair out from one of the tables just outside the café door and waited for her to sit before he took the other chair, both of them now facing the square. At this time of year an early lunch wasn't much of a success at the café, since the shadow of the church shaded this part of the square until half past twelve. But they'd arrived at the perfect time, basking in autumn warmth.

'I bet that's not true. I bet they do talk about you, but you're—'

'Titi! What can I get you? *Soupe du jour* is mushroom and gnocchi with parmesan. Oh, Lucas!' Jeanette Ta positioned herself between their chairs but paused no longer than it took her to blink. 'I'm so glad you two met. I've been meaning to introduce you since Tiana is afraid of spiders too...'

'I'm not afraid of spiders!' Lucas tried to look angry, but his tone betrayed him. 'One time! It spooked me, that's all.'

'Sure it did. Totally believe you. Still, I can't understand how it's taken you five years to meet one another. It's interesting. Just the other day, I said to Catherine—'

'I'll have the soup, please.' Tiana knew exactly where this was going. She should have known Jeanette was behind it somehow. Her friend had tried to set her up with just about every eligible man in the county at some point.

'No, that's not what I said. What else do you want?' Jeanette tapped her foot, but when Tiana answered, her expression changed from miffed to excited.

'I think I'll have the *mag*—'

'Oh, I haven't told you yet!' Jeanette was practically jumping up and down. 'I'm going to reopen the hotel! I'll finally have an establishment with an actual name. Not just "the *bar-tabac* in Saint-Maurice".'

Tiana felt her jaw drop. 'What? How? This place practically runs on government money.'

Hands flapping, Jeanette bobbed her head from left to right. 'I know, but that's because every village has their own little *bar-tabac*. If I want to make a profit, I need to think bigger.'

'But... how?'

'Well, there was this one person who was constantly' – Jeanette's hands were working overtime – 'in the way. But hey, not any more! So now we can go ahead. I have such amazing plans for the décor, and Théo has worked out the entire menu.'

'Still, though – how?'

'Oh.' The hands fell. 'I see. Well... I have an anonymous benefactor. Bit of a bummer. Wait, no, that doesn't work.' She pulled her mouth to one side. 'She's a bum? Lady? Bum lady? See, this is what happens when I try to crack a joke. Aha!' Her face brightened at the unexpected pun. 'I have the letter with the go-ahead right here. Want to see?'

She fished in the pocket of her apron, but when she pulled out an envelope, a balled-up sheet of paper came out too and fell to the ground.

Tiana and Lucas both bent down to pick it up. Her hand grazed his, and she looked up, finding his grinning face inches from hers. *This is it! Do not pull back!* Her cheeks heated all the way to her ears, but she kept her eyes where they were and even managed a smile. When he straightened first, holding the paper wad up to Jeanette, Tiana wasn't sure what made her happier, his proximity or the fact that she hadn't shied away from it.

Looking far too knowing and amused, Jeanette took the ball from Lucas.

'Another one of those public secret letters?' Lucas nodded towards the crumpled letter.

Jeanette shrugged. 'They're going around, aren't they? You get one?' The question was addressed to Tiana, who only realised it when she tore her gaze away from Lucas. By then he was answering for her.

'Yeah, it says she likes me. Now there's a secret I want to get to the bottom of.'

Jeanette wiggled her eyebrows. 'Maybe you should read her books and see just how deep that bottom lies.'

What?! Tiana's mouth dropped open. *She did not just say that. What will he think? What if he reads—*

Lucas reached out and touched her cheek. 'Hey, I liked you better with the blush.'

Well, he got what he asked for.

11

It's this whole murder business – very upsetting

Thibault tore off a piece of the baguette we'd just bought in the local supermarket at the edge of the village square. He obviously didn't care about food etiquette. Time to go home and get cooking. Lunch was late as it was and I was starting to get hangry.

'So, what have we learned?' He bit into the baguette.

'We've learned that the Madoras own a lot of penguins. They might have killed someone, or they might not have. Same with Mylène Grasset. Minus the penguins. Again, that is none of my business. My business is taking pictures of women with bright red lips. And since I have another client tomorrow, I only have this afternoon to talk to the estate agent, Laurent Tariel, and to Apolline Bailly.'

'Why only those two?'

'I don't know who else Jacqueline expects me to talk to!' It came out more frustrated than I'd intended. 'They are the only ones I know were in contact with La Mademoiselle. I can't go and talk to the entire village, hoping someone might let slip that they killed a person recently.'

'Sure you can.'

'Have you found a new place to stay yet?'

'Oh look, it's Tiana and Lucas. Lucas!'

Smooth.

Was it me, or were Lucas and Tiana not too happy to see us again? There seemed to be a reluctance in their steps towards us. Better things to do, would be my educated guess.

'Found your killer yet?' Lucas asked.

'No, and we're not looking.'

'Yes, we are, and I think you know more about it.'

All three of us stared at Beau, dumbstruck.

'I didn't kill anyone!'

Curious. I studied Lucas's face. His denial came out just a little too loudly. He seemed genuinely upset over Beau's dumb joke.

'I didn't say that. I said you know more than you let on. You said you didn't get a letter, but we reckon—'

'You reckon.' Don't drag me into this.

'—I reckon people who didn't get a letter this time have already had one earlier, and one of them is going to be the killer.'

'Beau...' I groaned. I seemed to be doing that a lot around him.

'Sounds to me like you're accusing me of murder.' Lucas was really getting angry. I didn't know where Beau was going with this, but he'd better cut it out quickly. Tiana's eyes were flitting back and forth between the two men. If Beau didn't stop this, she'd be holed up in her room seeking solace with fictional characters before you could say 'fight'.

'He's not. He's just hungry. Thibault, let's go.'

'But he's—'

'Okay, *I'm* hungry. Let's go.' I pushed him in the direction of my house.

That at last convinced him he was going too far. He pasted on his most boyish smile. 'Hey man, I'm just joking around. Enjoy your day. I need to cook for the angry lady.'

'I said hungry, not angry. And you wouldn't have to cook if you hadn't eaten everything I had in the house. You're already halfway through the bread we just bought.' As I talked, I kept shoving him forward, hoping that distance from this monkey would calm Lucas down. I'd apologise to Tiana later. 'Can you please stop eating long enough to learn some manners?'

We'd moved away far enough to be out of earshot. I glanced over my shoulder to be sure, before I swatted his arm. 'How could you not see he was getting mad?'

Thibault held up his palms. 'It was just a joke! Can I help it if he has no sense of humour?'

'You don't know him. Tiana really likes him. That doesn't happen very often. You should've been more careful.'

'I don't know Tiana either, but people normally like me. And my jokes.' He paused, then added in a low voice, 'And I don't eat that much.'

I could only shake my head at that.

He now pulled a sausage from our grocery bag and took out his pocket knife. 'Do you want me to cook?'

'Yes, please.' Food first, then the rest.

At lunchtime I was regretting that decision. If this was his ploy to make himself indispensable, it was working. Lunch was delicious. When I'd spooned the last of my chocolate mousse from the bowl, I leaned back in my chair. Beau was still attacking a Camembert. Which meant I must have eaten all the chocolate mousse. Oops.

'I'm still wondering how I'm going to talk to Tariel. Everyone in the village knows I'm not moving anywhere else any time soon. What reason could I have for talking to an estate agent?'

Mouth full of cheese, Thibault mumbled something, and I made a face.

'Didn't your *maman* tell you not to speak with your mouth full?'

He swallowed. 'I said, not a problem. You want me out of the house, right? So I'll need a new place. Best reason to talk to an estate agent.'

'I do want you out of the house. I also want you to stay out of my business.'

Before putting the next piece of cheese into his mouth, he huffed, 'Don't be so stubborn. I can help, so let me help.' In went the cheese.

So now *I* was being stubborn. Actually, with food in my stomach, I realised he might have a point. Which, of course, immediately put my hackles up. He wasn't supposed to be here to have that point in the first place! I crossed my arms, brooding over what I was going to say to the cheese-devouring model across the table. Instead, a different idea formed, but that would keep until tomorrow.

'Tariel's office doesn't open until two, and it is now...' I checked my phone. 'Already that. We're late. I don't want to show up at the Baillys' uninvited and around *goûter* time. I haven't even thought of an excuse to talk to her yet.'

Jacqueline owed me some wine after this. How could she expect me to talk to people I hadn't seen in years? People I had nothing in common with, except that we lived in the same village. She should have asked my mother. She was the mayor, she knew everyone. Maybe *I* should talk to my mother...

Beau rose and cleared the table. 'So do you want to wash up now or later?'

Wrinkling my nose at the dishes, I decided on a rinse-and-run.

Sock-less feet in brogues underneath a dark blue pinstriped suit, Laurent Tariel strutted around his office chest first, compensating for his lack of height with all the latest gadgets. Shiny black hair hung in curls around a face that emitted confidence verging on arrogance, but fingernails bitten to the quick betrayed his insecurity.

'Ah, Julietta, *chérie*. Selling after all?'

Before my aunt moved to the assisted living facility a few villages south-east of here, Tariel had been coming around, hoping to sell the place for her. Having promised the place to her favourite niece long ago, she knew his visits would make no difference, but she strung him along anyway. She was always a bit naughty. That was probably why I liked her so much in the first place. But for poor Tariel, it must have been a sour grape.

I wondered if he'd done a similar thing with La Mademoiselle. Only, she hadn't been planning to go anywhere, had she? The man with the answers was waiting for mine. Automatically, I pursed my lips and fluttered my eyelids.

'Still no, Monsieur Tariel. But I've brought you another little lamb.' I pushed Thibault forward, who extended his hand.

'Ah, a young professional moving away from the noise of the city, *non*? I have just the thing.' He went into full-on sales mode, and I zoned out. To Beau's credit, he fell into the role Tariel had attributed him without hesitation. I dreaded to think where he picked up those acting skills, but he was good.

'Oh, no, that won't do at all. Dusty little place. I have allergies – I need something neat and clean.'

They went through Laurent Tariel's entire catalogue, but everything was either too small, too dark, or too 'not him'. I knew Beau was playing a role, but part of me wondered how he was going to find his own place this way. How he was going to pay for it was his problem. I still had no idea what exactly he'd run away from, and if that included his job.

Also, none of this was getting us any closer to what we'd come for. While they were discussing housing, I wandered around the office, checking out advertised villas and flats, until I ended up near Tariel's desk. It was largely empty, save for a few neatly stacked forms in a basket. Not being the overly curious type, I turned to continue my stroll around the office, when my eye caught the name at the top of the form. Cyprien Gréban. My breath hitched, and I had to grab the corner of the desk to keep my knees from buckling. Couldn't be him. I panted. How many Cyprien Grébans could there be in the area? Air. I needed more air. Why wasn't there more air in this building?

'Julie? Julie!' Thibault appeared next to me, squeezing my shoulder. 'Calm down. Deep breaths, come on. In...'

In would be good. Air, in. Yes. I told myself to breathe in, which eventually I did.

'And out. Good. Again, in... And out. You okay?'

I nodded weakly.

Looking uncharacteristically concerned, Laurent Tariel handed me a glass of water.

As I drank, some logic returned to my thoughts. How was I going to explain this away? I could hardly tell them my ex-husband's best friend was going to—

'Murder,' I croaked. 'It's this whole murder business. Very upsetting.'

A tiny frown shot across Thibault's face, small enough that Tariel couldn't have noticed it, even if he had been looking at Beau. Which he wasn't. My remark had him nodding in understanding.

'Yes, it's been a shock to us all. No one expects such a thing to happen, especially in a quiet village like this.'

He seemed genuine enough. I took another sip to steady my voice. 'Won't your business suffer? Who would want to live here with a murderer on the loose?'

With a step away from me, he transformed back into the estate agent. 'We are within an hour's drive from Lyon, France's second biggest city after Paris, and arguably the better of the two to live and work in. But for anyone who prefers fresh air, birdsong, extensive views, and friendly neighbours, Saint-Maurice is the perfect place. Ten minutes from Villefranche, which has everything you could need, but without the noise and the pollution, Saint-Maurice is—'

'You don't have to sell it to me. I already live here.' I shouldn't have interrupted his pitch. I could almost see the thunderclouds gathering over his head.

'I'm glad you're feeling better, Julietta.'

Laying it on a little more thickly, I took a faltering, deep breath. 'With this murder, though, I might want to leave after all. I don't feel safe, really.' That thought seemed to perk him up a little. Would someone murder someone just to scare another someone away? I didn't think I had anything to do with this murder before, but how eager was Tariel to sell my house? I coughed to mask a giggle. Now I was just being ridiculous. 'At least that would free up another house. Like you said, the place is perfect, so I shouldn't think anyone would want to leave.'

Pinkie extended, Tariel put his index finger to his lips. 'There are plans to build new apartment buildings behind Moulin. Nothing is certain yet, but I don't think I'll be out of a job any time soon.' He winked, but he wasn't fooling me. The only house behind the neighbourhood of Moulin was that of La Mademoiselle. 'But for those who seek original features, there are still options. Not everyone leaves their house to their niece.'

That was most definitely a begrudging smile. The more he said, the less I liked him.

'I heard Claire Braymand had plans to leave before she was killed.' Now why did I say that? I wasn't getting anywhere, but this was a shot from here to Paris. Thibault narrowed his eyes, but I ignored him.

Tariel avoided looking at me. His casual had never been more casual. 'Really? I'd no idea.'

'She didn't mention it to you?'

His eyes cut to me. 'No. Not even when I went to talk to her about selling.'

I swallowed. Beau saved me by asking Tariel to keep him informed of anything new that might come up, and I practically ran out of there.

Lips pressed together, Thibault humphed at me. 'That could have gone better.'

'Yep,' I squeaked.

'You should have let me talk. I was well on my way to finding out more about him. Didn't you hear us?'

'Sorry, no.' I felt a little guilty, but I couldn't help seeing that name when I did.

'He wanted me to believe he has some kind of seedy contacts, but he showed no signs of recognition when I mentioned some of the region's biggest players. I could have found out why he was so eager to show off as a bad boy, but you just had to upstage me. That was some performance, by the way. How did you get so pale?'

I didn't answer. Beau would know why seeing Cyprien's name would upset me, but it suddenly struck me as too coincidental that he would show up after five years, around the same time Cyprien was thinking of coming here.

12

What if he took Franck's threat seriously?

Three thirty. I could just catch my mother before the *mairie* closed. Bracing myself, I pushed open the door to her office. I could always talk to my mother, and she usually either had some good advice or could at least calm me down, but there was a price: the I-told-you-sos were strong in this one.

A stack of papers hid most of her, but the hand-crocheted hairpiece in her salon-brown locks moved up when I entered, revealing smiling eyes behind reading glasses.

'Hello, Juju, good to see you.'

'Hi, *Maman.*' I pecked her on both cheeks, wondering where to begin, but she cut me off.

'Give me two seconds to finish this, and then I'm there for whatever trouble you've got yourself into now.' She didn't even look up, having established, as usual, what I came for within a minute of seeing me.

Trying to stay motionless, I waited for her to finish reading and signing the last of the stack. How there could be so much paperwork for a village of less than twelve hundred people would eternally astound me. But then, admin was something I did as little of as possible, so just the sight of such a mound of it was giving me the shivers.

With a final flourish *Maman* shifted the last sheet of paper and turned in her chair. 'Is this a biscuit kind of a problem or do we need chocolate?'

I weighed the question. Not a decision to be taken lightly. If I said biscuits, I might want the chocolate after I explained the situation. But I didn't want to say chocolate and blow the thing out of proportion. Was seeing Cyprien's name really chocolate-bad?

'Biscuits will do.' While *Maman* got up and pulled a tin from a drawer, I started my story with Thibault's arrival. Since she knew about Jacqueline's request, I skipped over my other activities of the day, ending up after half a biscuit at Tariel's. 'So that's why we ended up looking for a place for Beau to stay, and while he was talking, I noticed an application on Tariel's desk.' I took a bite of my biscuit for dramatic effect. 'It was Cyprien's, *Maman*. He wants to move here.'

My mother pursed her lips, tapping the tip of her reading glasses against them. 'And you think because Thibault came to you around the same time that the two events are related.' Letting her glasses dangle on their crocheted cord, she took a tiny bite of her biscuit. 'They might be. Or they might not be.

I think the most important aspect is whether either's reason for coming here has anything to do with you.'

'They're both connected to Franck. And he did threaten to kill me when he went to jail.'

Maman waved her biscuit through the air. 'Franck wouldn't kill anyone. Strictly white-collar crime – you said so yourself.'

'I know, but I'm not so sure about Cyprien. What if he took Franck's threat seriously? He'd do anything for him.'

'Taking another person's life is not something most people do lightly. And why would he wait four years? Also, why would he want to come and live here just to harm you?'

'Four years was Franck's sentence. You know he'll be released soon... I don't know, but there's already been one murder. What if it's all related? What if Cyprien sent me that letter?'

My mother raised her eyebrows.

'Oh, I didn't tell you, did I? You know how everyone has been getting these nasty letters about nothing, really? Mine said "I know about your husband".'

'Hm.' She took a bigger bite then. 'Mine said "you've been linked to fraud before". Since everybody knows that had nothing to do with me personally, I put it in the bin as soon as I read it.'

'As did I! But now I wonder... If Cyprien did write me that letter, he'd *really* know about my husband. What if he meant that he knew Franck is soon to be released and that it's not going to end well for me?' The hand holding the last of my biscuit began to shake, and *Maman* grabbed it.

'Look, half the village received one of these letters. Would he really go to all that trouble just to scare you? And he wouldn't know about all that goes on here. The letters all mentioned uncomfortable subjects, but nothing that wasn't already known. To the village in general, that is. Someone from Villefranche would never have known about all these things. No, we can safely assume the prankster is someone from the community, so you have no grounds for fear in that particular field.'

I took a deep breath. She was right, of course. I tried to remember all the calming things Jacqueline had told me after Franck uttered his death threat four years ago. Maybe I should have taken the offer for therapy, but after a while, I started to focus on building my business, and Franck's words seemed less threatening. He was still in jail. He couldn't get to me right now.

Except that his best friend was planning to move to my safe little village. 'Why would he come here, though? He loves the busyness of town, thinks the country is full of bugs put there specifically to taunt him. I can only think of one reason. Me.'

Popping the last of her biscuit in her mouth, she squeezed my hand. 'A lot can change in four years. He may have found a lovely girl who's helped him see the light.' I snorted, but *Maman* went on, 'Was there another applicant on the form?'

As much as I racked my brain, I couldn't remember. I shrugged. 'Maybe I could ask Laurent Tariel?'

Maman huffed. 'That man is as dirty as the top of a soap dispenser. I'm not sure he'd be the one to ask about any of your other criminal contacts.'

I shot her a look. She didn't mean that the way it sounded, but still... 'Beau thinks he's not connected at all.'

Pursing her lips again, *Maman* opened a drawer in her desk and pulled out her knitting bag. Ah, that meant she'd come to a conclusion, and the rest of the conversation would serve only to help me compose myself. Reading glasses perched once again on her nose, she took out a thin crochet needle and a barely visible thread and started to work it. 'You've always liked Thibault. It seems to me you still trust him. I also think you're making too much of your own involvement in this. Other than seeing Cyprien's name on a piece of paper, has anything actually happened to you?'

'Someone *was* murdered...'

'And this is connected to you, how?'

'Jacqueline asked me to talk to people.'

'Only this morning. That news can't have reached Cyprien, got him to form a plan, and execute it by applying to Laurent Tariel, all in these few hours.'

'So you think I'm okay?'

The craft work fell to her lap, and she looked me in the eye over her glasses. 'I really think you're safe, *ma fille*.'

If your mum says you're safe, you're safe, right? If only I were still a gullible child. I sighed.

'So have you been talking to people at all?' The crochet needle was back at work.

My earlier suspicion that my mother might have been the one setting up this whole 'talk to the village' thing for me worked itself back into my brain. Would Jacqueline have gone along with that, though?

'I've seen Marie Madora and Mylène Grasset. Think I'll go talk to Apolline Bailly next. According to Madame Durand, they used to be friends with La Mademoiselle.'

'Madame Bailly and Madame Braymand were friends, yes. Years ago. But I don't think talking to her will bring you any closer to finding the killer. Her husband, Corentin, is a CEO and a council member, you know. They're fine, upstanding citizens.'

I said the last words along with her in my head. Ever since I was young, my mother had had the Baillys on a pedestal the size of the Eiffel tower. Even when their son was charged with drunk driving, it was no more than a glitch. The parents were not to blame.

'But if you're going anyway, can you drop this off, please?' She pushed a folder across her desk towards me.

Ah! The perfect excuse. Thanks, *Maman*. 'If you insist.' I hesitated. 'Why didn't they ask you to talk to everyone? You know them. I don't. Not really, any more.'

'I'm the mayor. People will always be apprehensive or impressed when I talk to them. Strange, but true. You're relatively new, so it's only natural that you should ask questions.'

'Hm.' I got up and kissed her goodbye, my suspicion as good as confirmed.

I knocked on the door of the Bailly villa at precisely four o'clock. Not a very polite thing to do, arrive at *goûter* time uninvited and not bring anything. Then again, that was more of a children's thing anyway, and Apolline's son was long gone. I had an excuse for coming, but nothing for being invited in or prolonging the conversation. Part of me was already regretting not bringing Thibault. Maybe I could offer Apolline a free shoot too?

'Ah, Julie! How nice to see you. Come in, come in!'

Well, that was easy. Who needs you, Beau? '*Bonjour*, Apolline. I'm sorry for dropping in unannounced, but *Maman* wanted me to give this to you. Or to Corentin, probably.'

Quite a tall woman, Apolline Bailly never strayed from peak French fashion in her appearance. The middle parting ending in a formal chignon lengthened her slim face even more, and because she usually had her lips pressed together in disapproval of something or other, she always reminded me of the woman from that painting, *American Gothic*, even though her hair was dark.

She waved my apology away and led me into a living room the size of my entire ground floor. Pieces of modern art adorned the walls, but a huge window on my right stole the show. The view over the Saône valley was spectacular, Mont Blanc commanding the Alps in the distance. Though it was over a hundred miles away, it still looked majestic. Growing up here, I'd seen the view so often at different points inside and outside of the village that I'd got used to seeing it. La Grande Maison, the stately home that had been in our family forever and was now occupied by my brother, oversaw a similar area, but this villa was situated higher up, making the view even more expansive.

There was something else, though. The Baillys' garden was one of the most luscious I'd ever seen. Even well into autumn, the flowers they'd planted provided an explosion of colour. I recognised seasonal favourites, but some of the plants were unfamiliar to me.

'It's always the first thing people see,' Apolline said with some pride, 'And eventually, it's what sold the house to us. We've lived here for over fifteen years, and I still take time to enjoy it almost every day.'

'It's beautiful,' I agreed. I stretched my hand out with the folder my mother had given me, but Apolline didn't take it.

'Leave it on the table, would you? I have to take a blackberry clafoutis out of the oven, and then I want you to tell me all about your little business.' With that she left the room.

I blinked. Lovely. People paid me handsomely for a shoot. Maybe I should call myself the CEO of my business to be able to rank on her scale of importance. I shook my head, plucked the nasty thought out of my head, and looked around for a spot to dump it. Can't leave that negativity lying around just anywhere, you know. A large cactus in the far corner drew my eye. Perfect. A dry spot for my negativity to shrivel up in. Dropping the file on the table, I moved closer to the cactus. We all have our little sillinesses, but I didn't want mine to put Apolline off talking. What if she saw me aiming my imaginary negativity at her cactus? Better to get closer and drop it in while pretending to admire the plant.

'Isn't it gorgeous?' There. See? It had worked. 'It's my husband's hobby, really. He collects cacti from all over the world. I've learned to love them too. And other succulents. But he's the expert. Whenever we go on holiday, we travel to places that have cacti we don't yet possess. Very educational. Some of them are quite rare.'

I nodded along with an interested smile, expecting her to list all the fascinating places she'd been to, but I was spared for now. Apolline put a plate of delicate snacks on the coffee table and invited me to sit.

'I've been meaning to talk to you,' she continued what I was starting to believe would be a monologue. 'We were so excited to hear you'd be moving back to Saint-Maurice. And bringing another business with you. These small villages have so little to offer these days. But we are dedicated to making the most of it. As a community, you see? Do you have any plans for the community?'

What was this, a job interview? 'Erm...'

'It's so important for all of us to stick together. We feel everyone should carry their weight, don't you? Of course, some of us weigh more than others, if you see what I mean, but as a community, we can divide that weight among us and come out as equals. More or less.'

What was she on about?

'So that's why I wanted to talk to you. We feel it's important to know what goes on in the village, so that we can act upon any irregularities.'

Hello, secret police. Had she always been like this? Her son was quite a bit younger than me, so I hadn't really known her well before I left, other than from my mother's cooing. 'These must be difficult times for you, then.'

She blinked, her head to one side like a pigeon. 'How do you mean?'

'With the murder and the letters? Or do you already know who did it?' I bit my lip. Last time I'd been direct, it hadn't worked.

Apolline Bailly made a face as if she'd smelled my negativity in her potted cactus. 'No, of course I don't. It's very distressing. Although – and I don't mean this in a negative way, mind – if anyone was to be murdered, it would have been her.'

I took a cracker with some pâté off the plate to hide the fact that I had nothing to say to that. How could anyone take those words in a positive way?

I made an ambiguous noise, and Apolline continued, 'She used to do good with her knowledge of what went on. But what do you expect when you try to turn that knowledge into something profitable?'

Mmm, good cracker. Wait, profitable? 'Mine simply said, "I know about your husband". No demands or anything.'

Apolline flinched. 'No... no, that's not what I meant. She must have sent the letters because she was the only one... I mean, the only one nasty enough to send them. You see?'

I wanted to kick myself. I'd given her my information, instead of finding out more about her letter. I was not cut out for being an investigator! Curses on my mother and Jacqueline for making me do this. I took a deep breath. The negativity would have to be expelled by air since I couldn't very well pluck something from my head right in front of Upstanding Citizen.

Time to change tactics. 'I wonder what will happen to her house. I do hope the new people will be a good addition to the community.'

Bingo. Her face lit up. 'Don't you worry about that. She had no family and she'd lost all her friends, so the land will revert to the state. And I don't mind telling you that we have big plans for it.'

Now for the big question: should I stop, or could I feed this enthusiasm? 'It's a shame there's already a house there. It would be a prime location for an apartment building, wouldn't it?'

Apolline all but clapped her hands. 'I like the way you think. Luxurious apartments would bring in exactly the right sort of people, don't you think?'

Depends on your definition of 'right'. 'So it's actually rather convenient that she died.'

Aannnd I'd ruined it. Her face fell. No doubt she felt she'd said too much. I wondered if I could pull a Beau to save the situation. 'But what I came here for, in the spirit of community, is to offer you a shoot.'

She raised her eyebrows, not looking flattered in any way.

'You know, at my studio?'

She stood up and indicated a large painting of what looked like the trunks of a bunch of birch trees. 'Have you seen this?'

It would be difficult *not* to see it. The thing was at least two by three metres.

'It's by an up-and-coming German painter. That one there' – bits of overlapping scrap metal – 'is from a highly sought-after Portuguese artist. Note that none of our pieces represent the human form.' The corners of her mouth pulled down even further. 'Frankly, I've no desire to bare any part of mine.'

That would be a no, then. Having disgusted her long enough, I decided it was time to go and stood up. 'Well, that's all I have to offer. Thank you for your hospitality. I must say, that clafoutis smells divine.'

Her features softened, which released some of the tension that had crept into my shoulders. Though I didn't care about what Apolline thought of me, I knew my mother would have something to say if I had appeared rude to her local idol.

'Thank you. This time of year, I always make sure to pick some blackberries. Nature's way of saying, "Thanks for being French. Have some more food to prepare".' She laughed, but then her face turned serious again. 'I was going to pick mushrooms this week with Laura – Laura Durand,' she added by way of explanation. 'She always accompanies me on these little excursions. It's so lovely to be able to share one's knowledge. But I don't think she's up to it now. Shame.'

I said goodbye with a repeat invitation, should she change her mind. I knew that would leave her with a sour taste, but I just couldn't help myself. And then I realised I was already looking forward to telling Thibault about it.

13

Why are you here?

Could I trust Thibault, though? According to my mother, I was perfectly safe, and seeing threats where there weren't any. I'd had no distrust of Beau before, but then I hadn't seen him in five years. What if, instead of escaping, he'd joined the family? Maybe Jacqueline just hadn't caught on to his illegal activities yet. He'd already flaunted his acting skills. What if he was using them against me?

I pressed my eyes closed and immediately stumbled over some loose gravel on the road. The Bailly villa was located well outside the village. A path that started close to my brother's Grande Maison and ended at the nearest crossroads to the Bailly villa ran up the hill through the woods. But to reach it, I had to go along the asphalt road for a bit.

'To heck with healthy step counts. Next time I'm taking my car again.'

My thoughts kept coming back to Thibault and whether he knew about Cyprien's imminent move to Saint-Maurice.

Only one thing for it. I'd have to ask him. Of course, the next question that popped up was what I'd do with either answer. If he did know, was that necessarily bad? Not according to my mother.

By the time I'd reached my front door, frustration was running high. Especially when Beau opened my personal front door before I'd even found my key.

'Where have you been?'

'Why are you in my house?'

'You let me stay here, don't you remember? I didn't think you were that old.'

I silenced him with my dirtiest look and stepped around him. Throwing my bag on the kitchen table, I wheeled round and threw my words at him. 'Why are you here?'

All puzzled innocence, he held his palms up. 'I told you, I escaped.'

'Not good enough. You didn't even ask your best friend for a bed. You came directly to me. Why.' It wasn't even a question any more, it was a demand.

A shadow fell over Beau's handsome face – one that suddenly made him look older. I quelled an attempt at levity with a narrowing of my eyes, and he sighed, shoulders drooping.

'Julie, there's... I...' He paused long enough for me to wonder whether he was making something up. 'Believe it or not, you're my safe space. I tried to get out before, but that time I did go to Gío. They threatened me, him, his business… Anything they could think of. In the end, I had to go back. But with you, that wouldn't work. It'd be too obvious.'

I could believe that. But he knew I could believe it. Would I allow myself to? The more I thought about it, the more difficult the decision became. Did I really want to see him as my enemy? Or would I be a fool to trust him?

His eyes pleaded with me, less boy and more man than five minutes before.

'How am I supposed to know whether that's true? You can't prove it.'

'No.'

That's all I had. And I really wanted to believe him. Against my better judgement maybe. 'I still don't want you in my house,' I grumbled.

He grinned, back to his own age in less than half a second. 'You didn't leave me any biscuits.'

It took me a little longer to recover, still fighting myself on the decision to trust him for now, but his airy smile soon cleared the atmosphere. 'I don't have any biscuits. If you want some, you'll have to bake them.'

'I don't bake.' He wrinkled his nose as if even the thought stank.

I ducked into a cupboard and pulled out some dessert chocolate that I slammed on the table along with a chopping board. 'Chop!'

With a mock salute, he set to work removing the wrappers and attacking the chocolate with the biggest knife he could find. 'You want to know what I think?'

'No.' I really didn't.

'We're going about this all wrong. It's obvious that someone has been sending fake letters to mask the real letters La Mademoiselle sent.'

'Is it?'

'Is it what?'

'Obvious.'

'Isn't it? Think about it – La Mademoiselle Braymand sends out nasty letters. One of her victims kills her, but to make sure they don't stand out somehow, they send everyone else a letter too.'

I considered his words. All of that had crossed my mind too, especially after Apolline nearly confirmed it. He'd apparently given the matter much more intelligent thought than I would have given him credit for. 'I think it's too soon to say anything with certainty. But that does seem to be the most likely scenario.'

'So can we discount everyone with a fake letter?'

'Certainly not. But I'm not here to find out who did it. I only need to talk to people.'

'Yes, but since you're so reluctant, why not just talk to the ones who might actually have done it? For that reason, Maarten and Marie Madora are still on my list. They didn't get a fake letter, so they probably got a real one.'

'That's too quick an assumption. Perhaps the killer didn't know who'd already had a letter. There may well be people with two letters and some with none. *If* there were more original victims in the first place. If La Mademoiselle did start this whole thing, she may have only sent one letter to one person, and that person didn't know he was the only one. Besides, the whole point of these letters is to make sure they're secret, right? So why would the killer assume he'd be found out?'

'Or she.' He popped a piece of chocolate into his mouth, thinking as he chewed. 'Panic?'

'Bit of a long panic, if they're going through the trouble of writing a letter to most of the village.' Mixing the ingredients for chocolate chip cookies together, I added, 'So I went to see Apolline Bailly.'

He didn't look up. 'Ah?'

'She has got to be the best suspect yet. She went on about community, and how important it is for a councilman to know what's going on in the village. She's also terrible with secrets. It was obvious she couldn't tell me, but something was waiting to burst from her lips. I think it's a good thing for her husband that this is such a tiny village. The council must not have that many important secrets here. If it had, I'm sure Corentin would think twice before telling his wife.'

'Oh, we're calling them suspects now, are we?' His grin was so obviously meant to disarm me. I wished it wouldn't work so well!

I smiled. 'All right, fine, have it your way. Seriously though, she is the perfect suspect. She could barely keep in that she'd had a letter she knew was sent by La Mademoiselle. That would fit in neatly with your theory of more than one letter writer. And also with the fact that she was poisoned by licking envelopes.'

'So she ticks all the boxes.'

'Hm.' I paused. 'If only she wasn't so obvious about it! I mean, she told me she didn't like the woman, she already has plans for her property, *and* she goes foraging with Laura Durand, so she knows which plants she can pick and which are bad for you. If you were the killer, would you tell me any of those things?'

'Maybe she's just not the criminal mastermind? Killers don't have to be geniuses, you know.' He finished chopping the chocolate and added it to my bowl.

Stirring on autopilot, I continued, 'Maybe it's a double bluff. She's relying on her status as an Upstanding Citizen to keep her away from suspicion.'

'Do you know who the police suspect?'

'No.' I slid the bowl onto the table. 'But I'm starting to wonder if they needed me for their investigation at all. I talked to my mother before I went over to Apolline, and I think she and Jacqueline came up with this hare-brained scheme to get me to talk to my neighbours. She – my mother – has been nagging me to get more involved in village affairs. After talking to Apolline, I don't wonder why.' I growled in frustration, and rapped the bowl of dough with my wooden spoon. 'This needs to go in the fridge, but I need cookies now. It can sit in the fridge until the oven heats up.' I slumped on a chair.

'I'll do that for you, shall I?' Beau asked, picking up the bowl and placing it in the fridge. Then he turned the oven on. 'Does it matter, though?'

'What do you mean?'

'If they only asked you to talk to people to get you to talk to people, don't you still want to find out who did it?'

I'd already opened my mouth to say no, but didn't I really? The more I talked to these people, the more curious I got as to who would have it in them to take a life. It didn't really make me want to become part of the community, knowing one of them was a murderer, but if I could help put the killer behind bars... Would it put me in a better light with the rest of them? I stared at Beau, thinking out loud. 'I honestly don't know who else I'd need to talk to. Unless someone sneaked into the house unseen, I've already talked to everyone who had some sort of connection to La Mademoiselle.'

'You don't think one of them did it?'

I shrugged, counting on my fingers. 'Marie Madora doesn't seem to have a motive at all. Neither does Mylène Grasset. Laurent Tariel admits that he went to talk to La Mademoiselle about selling her house, but I don't see him murdering an old lady just to get a commission on the sale of her land. And Apolline... I don't know.'

'She's the only one with the plant knowledge, right?'

'Yes, and as far as I can see, she did have a motive, but it still doesn't seem to fit. For instance, she hasn't been inside that house for years. So who else is there?'

'Lucas.'

I swatted at his arm. 'Are you still on that?'

'He knew the plants.'

'He's a gardener.'

'So?'

'So of course he knows the plants! But he wouldn't have offered up the knowledge if he was guilty, would he?'

'Double bluff? Didn't you notice how he keeps avoiding answering the letter question?'

I stared again. Now that I thought about it, Thibault was right. 'I'm not talking to Lucas. Who else would know about the poisons?'

'Don't ask me, I don't know these people.'

'You're quick enough to accuse them of murder, though.'

He shrugged.

'I suppose there are several people in the village who know enough about plants,' I continued. 'Madame Dufaux, for instance, and Lily. You don't know her, but she takes people foraging for mushrooms in autumn, complete with wild salad. Catherine, Tiana's neighbour. Have you met her yet?'

Thibault shook his head.

I tapped my lip. 'But I don't think any of them have a connection to Claire Braymand, so no motive to kill her. I wonder what was in the original letters. Or letter. But that's a secret that could go back years.'

'It must have been bad, though, if after all this time, they'd still want to shut her up badly enough to kill her. Do you think maybe it wasn't their first murder?' Beau's eyes shone again, but my hand went to my stomach.

'I don't even want to consider that.' I sighed. 'You know what, I give up. Let's just finish these cookies, and do you want tea?'

He wanted the beer he had in his own fridge, and he didn't want cookies any more. I reminded him that he was moving out the day after, which he ignored, and we parted ways for the day, me finishing and somehow eating three of my cookies.

I thought about calling Jacqueline and letting her know what I thought of her scheme, but ended up going through my work emails instead, with a bowl of yesterday's mushroom soup next to my computer. I'd call Jacqueline in the morning, and that would be the end of the whole matter. If she hadn't asked me to talk to people I'd normally steer clear of, I wouldn't have suspected Beau of anything untoward in the first place.

There was still a little niggling residue of doubt in the pit of my stomach. I didn't want it there. I wanted to trust Beau and be his friend when he needed me. But wasn't it awfully coincidental that two people from my past showed up in my village at practically the same time?

Ugh! I could go on like this forever. I had to make a decision, and my decision was to help Beau out and trust him. I leaned back in my chair, satisfied with my determination. Upstairs, Beau was moving around, making the floorboards creak their approval. He'd only be here for one more night anyway. What could possibly happen?

I gathered my things together, switched off my computer, and returned to the kitchen via the courtyard. As I washed my soup bowl, I glanced through the kitchen window at the twilight outside. A black car pulled up in the driveway. Who would come and see me at this hour? I went through the list of people I knew who owned black cars, but since cars don't interest me very much, I couldn't even think of one.

I dried my hands and waited for the sound of the knocker, but nothing came. When I looked out again, the driver had left the vehicle, but he or she had obviously gone to my studio door. In that case, Thibault would send them over, and I'd hear them knock in about thirty seconds. I waited. Nothing. Now I know I said I'm not the curious type, but this kind of thing gets even me going. Since the sink and worktop were in the way, I couldn't see much from the kitchen window, so I went upstairs to the guest room.

Hiding behind my curtains, I felt like a snooping old lady. But this was my house. I was entitled to know what was going on. The owner of the car turned out to be Laurent Tariel. Though Thibault was still inside, and thus out of my line of vision, he must have opened the door because Tariel was gesturing and smiling. I couldn't hear what he said, but he looked much more relaxed than he'd been in his office. I wondered whether they'd notice if I cracked open the window, so I could eavesdrop on their conversation.

Then Tariel looked up, straight at the window where I was hiding. His gaze searched the entire front of the house before he reached into his pocket and handed Beau a... something. What was that? My imagination ran amok. Drugs? That's what shady characters did, right? Couldn't have been much, though. Whatever it was, it was quite small. Besides, Beau and drugs? Would he really have sunk that low?

Maybe it was... what? Instructions? Like in a heist movie? Money! But Tariel giving Thibault money made no sense. Then again, Tariel giving Thibault anything made no sense. What Beau had said about the estate agent not being in the know about the local baddies made it obvious that they didn't know each other. Unless, again, those acting skills were being used against me. Had I not decided only fifteen minutes ago that I was going to trust Thibault? I'd shared all my thoughts about what was going on. Now, that didn't seem like such a good idea after all.

Laurent Tariel laughed, making a wide gesture indicating my house and studio, and waving as if throwing the lot over his shoulder. How dare he deride my property like that! He hadn't been so disdainful when he'd wanted to sell it. But now I was starting to wonder if my house was on some kind of smugglers route or something. Maybe I should start paying attention to what happened around here at night, after everyone had closed their shutters.

Tariel drove off, and I sank down on the guest bed. Thinking about it logically, most of my earlier thoughts seemed outrageous, worthy of Isabel Cochon and her buried treasure. But the fact remained that Tariel seemed awfully friendly with someone he supposedly only met that afternoon. And then there was the link to Cyprien Gréban. No matter how much I shivered, I couldn't shake the feeling that something was seriously off. Not only did 'my' village harbour a murderer, but now I might have let a threat into my own home. I closed the shutters, wondering if it was too late to keep the bad things out.

14

So where's my kiss?

Something was definitely wrong. Whether it would turn out to be him or her, Tiana hadn't decided. But the whole day had been almost too perfect. She was already wondering whether he'd kiss her goodnight, and they'd only just finished their pizza.

After they saw Julie and Beau in the square that afternoon, Tiana had been worried that the spell had been broken, the way Lucas reacted. His grumpiness had had no grounds, and afterwards, he seemed nervous. Tiana had taken it as a good sign, though, that he'd be nervous as to what she thought about him. She'd been a little extra cheery, and his strange behaviour had fallen away.

They'd wandered off into the country, and soon he was showing her all kinds of plants and telling her how these little things she'd taken for granted all had their own special uses and tricks to survive. His enthusiasm had made her want to learn more about nature, something she'd never considered before.

They'd passed a heap of fermenting grape skins, dumped there after the juice had been pressed out to become the famous Beaujolais wine. The smell had been so strong that they'd fled to a nearby field, laughing and joking about his name sounding the same as the French expression for yuck, *beurk*.

But now he was ranting about something silly. What was it again? Maybe she should pay attention.

'I didn't like it,' Lucas was saying. 'I mean, that's not Captain America, that's Captain Barista. And it's just the one film too.'

'Absolutely. Clean-shaven all the way.'

'Right?' He laughed. He had a good laugh. All rumbly. Tiana gave herself a mental slap. What was she, one of her heroines?

'Listen, I keep early hours, so can I walk you home?'

Tiana almost pouted. Today had been amazing. Not once had he let on that he was bored or wanted to get away. Not even when she started explaining the finer details of the romantic suspense novel she'd been working on! It was almost as if he was really interested. 'Okay. I had fun today,' she added, immediately regretting her corniness.

'Yeah, me too. It's been a great day.'

'Even when Julie accused you of being distracted in her studio?'

He laughed again, sending flutters through Tiana's stomach. 'You have to admit, she has the most distracting studio. But I was only thinking of plants. Scout's honour.' He held up three fingers and placed his other hand over his heart. 'I still think it's odd that the police would involve a civilian in their investigations, though.'

'Ha! For one, the detective in charge is her friend, so for two, she knows Julie is desperately curious. She would have probably found a way to insert herself into the proceedings, even if they'd tried to keep her out.'

'And you're not? Curious, I mean.' The way he said it sounded very curious indeed. Was he trying to find out more about her character? They were about halfway up the path to Tiana's house, and it was quickly getting dark. Maybe she could persuade him to stay a little longer to find out.

'Na. I have no trouble staying away from everything. If I want excitement, I'll make it up and write it down. Do you want to sit for a bit?' She indicated the bench in front of her house and hoped twilight would hide the deep heat she felt in her cheeks.

He grinned and sat next to her. 'You don't want to find out who the killer in your village is?'

Her eyes opened wide. 'No! Surely it can't be someone from the village? I assumed she'd surprised a burglar or something.'

'Who poisoned her with her own envelopes?'

'Oh. Right. See, I hadn't even thought about it any more, and now you've scared me. If someone is going after women who live on their own, I could be next!'

He grinned. 'Stick to email for now.'

'Ha. Ha.'

'I wouldn't worry. Unless you've been nasty to someone lately.'

'I'm not anything to anybody. I'm just here, writing.'

'I think you're pretty nice.'

Did he have to keep making her blush? He seemed to make a sport out of it. There was a definite smirk around his lips, but he changed course and asked, 'So why romance?'

She fidgeted with one of her fingernails. 'The short version, or the long one?'

'Whichever you prefer.'

Biting her lip, she studied his face. He did ask. 'Happy endings. The true love forever my parents never had. There was a time I believed it only happened in books, so that's where I escaped to.'

Lucas was silent for a long beat, staring at the ground. 'That's not such a long story.'

She shrugged. 'I'm sure you can imagine the long story behind it.'

'Hm,' was all he said, nodding slightly. 'Did, ehm... I mean...' He looked up, catching her gaze. 'I...'

What? He looked so forlorn all of a sudden. 'It was a long time ago, though. It doesn't bother me now.' Well, not directly, anyway.

Unfortunately, her words didn't seem to make a difference to his change of spirit. He held her gaze for a moment or two, then cast his eyes down to the ground again. When he looked up, there was a fake smile on his lips. 'That's good.' He rose. 'I'll let you get on with your evening. Thank you for spending the day with me, Ti. I really had a great time.'

Exactly, so where's my kiss? She got up as well, not really sure why they were now standing.

He took her hand and kissed it gently.

That was... sweet? What century were they in?

'I'll be next door tomorrow, so I guess I'll see you then.'

'Yes,' was all she could say before he left. Tiana stood staring at his back for a second. What had happened? What had she said? Was it the romance thing? If he didn't want to know, he shouldn't have asked.

Questioning her sanity, Tiana went inside, and turned on a few lamps. Then she found herself standing in the middle of the room, letting out a crazy giggle. She hadn't done anything wrong. His behaviour was just plain weird!

Of course, two seconds later she was questioning that again, deciding afterwards that it was not her, it was him. She went through the cycle for another fifteen minutes, but then shook her head and turned on the TV. Some film about shoes couldn't hold her attention, but it did remind her of something. She picked up her phone, and sent off a text to Laura Durand.

I still have your boots. Want me to drop them off tomorrow, or do you need to keep them secret?

The film ended and Tiana went to bed, shaking her head. Two seconds later, she got up and double-checked all her locks. It couldn't be someone from the village, really. But she'd thought she knew everyone before, and then she met a man who'd lived here for five years. There could easily be others she didn't know. People less nice. Nice but odd. Next time she'd make sure she'd get her kiss.

15

I've looked everywhere!

My alarm clock went off at eight. I swatted at it, not ready to start the day. Lots of things to do that I didn't want to think about yet. Tell Jacqueline I didn't want to snoop any more. Tell Beau he'd have to leave, unless, according to the brilliant idea I had yesterday, he'd let me photograph him. After what I saw last night, though, I wasn't so sure letting him stay another night was as brilliant as I'd thought. Maybe I should just go back to sleep. But I also had a shoot today, which perked me up enough to get out of bed. I did love my job.

Coffee in hand, I was just getting ready for a bakery run when a loud rap on the front door startled me. A sweaty, nervous man stood panting in the doorway. I hardly recognised him. It could have been Monsieur Durand, but nothing about him was 'just so' any more. This person wore wrinkled trousers, half of his shirt had come free of his waistband, a purplish black substance stained his shoes, and his hands... At first I thought they were scratched, but Durand was wringing his hands around a red-tipped pen, colouring them even more.

'She's gone!' he wailed. 'I can't find her. I've looked everywhere!'

It didn't take much imagination to find out who he meant. Where could his wife have gone? Especially in the state she was in. No wonder Monsieur Durand was distraught. I invited him in and sat him down at the kitchen table with a cup of coffee and one of my cookies. He kept muttering unintelligible half-sentences and wiping his brow with his dirty hands until I asked him, 'When did you last see her?'

A shaking hand went to his lips. 'Last night. She wasn't... feeling very well, so I brought her up to bed. I went down again because it was too early for me to join her, but then when I did go up, she... she wasn't there and...' The tone of his voice rising, Monsieur Durand tightened his grip on the coffee cup so much that the handle snapped off. If it were anyone else, I would have hugged them or at least touched their arm, but to prim Monsieur Durand, that might be the last straw. He stared at the broken handle as if he was watching water burn but forgot to apologise. 'I was up all night calling her friends and looking for her outside. Do you think I should call the police?'

I nodded. 'I think that might be wise. I have a friend with the force – let me call her for you.'

The call I'd imagined that morning was quite different from the one I now made. Instead of telling her I was done helping, I was asking her for help. With Jacqueline on her way over, I turned back to Monsieur Durand, who was still shaking, but his breathing had calmed down.

'I don't know what to do,' he whimpered. 'I don't...'

I took the chair next to him. 'Tell me where you've been. Maybe I can think of another place to look.'

After a faltering sip of coffee, he swallowed hard. 'I went upstairs around eleven and when she wasn't there, I first looked in the kitchen, then the bathroom, and the rest of the house. When she wasn't anywhere in the house, I started to get concerned. I looked in the garden, but she wasn't there either. She didn't answer when I called out...' His lip quivered, and he took a deep breath. I expected him to continue, but he sipped his coffee, interspersed with more deep breaths.

Deciding to leave the questioning to Jacqueline, I let Monsieur Durand sip his coffee in relative peace. Poor man. And poor woman. What could have possessed her to leave the house without telling her husband? And where could she have gone? Other than Thibault's meeting with Laurent Tariel, I hadn't heard anything last night. But then our houses were separated by a field owned by Auguste, who lived on the other side of the Durands. When a knock on the door announced Jacqueline, Monsieur Durand hadn't said any more.

I let Jacqueline into the kitchen, but upon seeing her, Monsieur Durand only started to shake even more, saying he didn't want to make a fuss over nothing. Before I could remark that losing your wife does not count as nothing, Jacqueline dealt with him in a more professional manner. That was my cue to leave it to her and make more coffee, as her partner, Marc Froment, was also on his way. When Beau burst in at the same time as Froment, the chaos was more or less complete. Poor Monsieur Durand trembled like a trapped rabbit.

'Thibault, I think we should leave Monsieur Durand and the officers alone.'

'No!' Durand shot up. 'Please. I'd like you to stay.'

I eyed Jacqueline, who nodded, so I pulled Beau off to the side, where we leaned against the counter while Jacqueline started her questioning. The first bits I already knew, but I had to admit I was getting curious to know the rest.

'By that time I was quite worried, you see. My first thought was to call her mother, but she lives too far away, and I didn't want to worry her. It was also getting rather late. I'm afraid I didn't check the clock, but it must have been close to midnight.'

Marc Froment's pen darted across his pad. I wondered what he put down. 'Worried... call mother... too far... midnight.' Something like that. Or would it be more in the vein of 'Suspect appears to be nervous. Or perhaps he hasn't had breakfast'. I hadn't had any breakfast. Should I offer something to everyone? Maybe I'd run into Laura Durand at the bakery. She must get hungry at some point too.

'I called her phone, but it went straight to voicemail. Then I... waited.' He quickly glanced at both detectives, before fixing his gaze back on the table. 'I thought she might have gone for a walk and she'd be back soon. I'm afraid I fell asleep, but when I woke up, she still hadn't returned. I've been out looking for her since six this morning, but I didn't find her on any of the paths she usually takes.' His tone rose again, and his tempo picked up. 'And now I don't know what to do any more. I don't!'

'We will have a look ourselves, Monsieur Durand. If needs be, we'll organise a search party, but for now, if you don't mind, we'd like to visit your house and garden.' Jacqueline's calm voice seemed to settle Durand. The groove between his eyebrows was still there, but he'd stopped trembling, staring instead at my friend. 'Is that all right, Monsieur Durand?' she asked more explicitly.

He jumped, letting go of most of his anxious behaviour. '*Oui*. Yes, of course. Will you give me some time to tidy? I'm afraid I haven't cleared away anything since yesterday.'

'That won't be necessary, Monsieur Durand. We won't judge you. All we are concerned with is finding your wife.' Marc Froment stood, holding out his hand in an invitation to Durand to lead the way. Letting go of his broken coffee cup,

Durand went back to wringing his hands, this time without the red pen in between. I found it on the floor after they'd left. Jacqueline winked at me, mouthing 'talk later' as she passed. Indeed we would. Maybe she could explain what exactly it was that felt off about this whole thing.

Miraculously, Thibault had managed to stay silent all this time. Not any more, though.

'This is how you stay out of police business?'

I slapped at his arm. 'Go make yourself useful and get us some fresh bread.'

'With pleasure.' He grinned and sauntered off.

Trust him? I wasn't sure. But until I was, my life would be much easier if I at least pretended to. I watched him go through the kitchen window. Walking in the direction of the village, he would pass the Durands' house. Poor Laura. What could have happened? In my head I replayed the conversation I'd had with her two days before. Like me, she'd felt like an outsider. And, of course, finding Claire Braymand like that must have been quite a shock. Enough to make her wander off?

If only I'd invested a little in getting to know my neighbours. I'd thought there would be time for that later. Perhaps I could have come up with a place to look for her if I'd known her better. As things were, I couldn't even console her husband. What *was* his first name?

Wait, someone had told me yesterday that they went foraging with Madame Durand. Who was that? Apolline. Hm. Did I really want to call her? Monsieur Durand had probably done that already, anyway. He said he was up all night calling her friends. Still, it was the one thing I felt I could do for Laura.

One good thing about coming back to the village you grew up in: you already have everyone's number. I tapped in Apolline's name and mentally braced myself.

'*Oui, allô?*'

'It's Julie. I assume you heard about Laura's disappearance?'

An audible gasp on the other end. Oops. I might have sugar-coated that a bit.

'I'm sorry, Apolline, I thought you knew. Monsieur Durand said he called her friends, and you said yesterday that you went foraging with her.'

Apolline's voice was hoarse. 'Yes... yes, I was... I mean I *am* her friend. I'll be right over.'

She hung up before I could protest. Jacqueline would have to deal with her. And then I'd have to deal with Jacqueline. I winced.

With a sigh, I pulled up my calendar on my phone. My client would be here at two. It was nearly ten now, which gave me four hours to lay out the poses I thought would suit her best. I also still had Beau's bike, which I should definitely use to the fullest as long as it was here. That's assuming Beau hadn't suddenly found somewhere else to stay after all, but my instincts said he was counting on me developing some kind of soft spot for him that would change my mind. Unfortunately for him, there were no soft spots. When it came to defending my male-free zone, I would gladly man the cannons. I mean woman the cannons... Defend. That's what I'd do.

Whistling a jaunty tune, the object of my grumpy thoughts came strolling in, bakery bag under his arm. 'Some haughty dame in a Mercedes just pulled up next door, demanding to see the officer in charge. I think your friend sent her packing.'

His last words were accompanied by yet another knock on my door.

I groaned. 'Here we go.'

'Julie?' Apolline's high voice reverberated through the thick wooden door before I'd had time to open it.

'Morning, Apolline.'

Her stilettos clicked past me on the painted tiles of my hallway. 'You won't believe those detectives! They asked me to wait! They have no idea who I am.'

I feigned shock. 'You must have told them.'

'They wouldn't even listen!' She perched on a kitchen chair, eyeing Thibault and then me suspiciously.

'This is my assistant, Thibault.' Hm, that was starting to roll off my tongue annoyingly easily. 'Would you mind if we have some breakfast? With all that's been going on today, we haven't had the chance yet.'

Apolline's hand fluttered in an if-you-must gesture. Looked like her thundercloud wasn't done unloading. 'Do you know what happened?' It was almost an accusation. I was going to lie to keep the peace, but Thibault had other plans.

'Oh yes, we were the first to know. Julie is very well connected, both in high and low places. She's almost a double agent. Anything happens around here, she's the first they come to.' He took a big bite of his croissant, leaving Apolline staring. First at him, then at me.

I wrapped my own mouth around a croissant to keep from laughing. I wondered what this would do for my standing in the village.

'Oh,' was all that came out of Apolline's mouth. 'Well.'

I took pity on her. 'I'm sure they'll fill you in soon. In the meantime, now that you're here, would you like to see my studio?'

She blinked once or twice, but then accepted my offer.

Still chewing on my croissant, though careful not to leave a trail of buttery flakes, I led her across the courtyard to my White Palace. As expected, Apolline showed some difficulty in remaining polite, remarking only on the good quality of my furniture, but her mouth was a thin line whenever she glanced at my poster-sized work.

'And finally, here is my office.' I opened the door, witnessing her expression go from mildly unbored to bulging eyes when she saw the large price list I had up on my wall.

'People actually pay you this much for a picture of their bottom?'

Standard reaction. I gave her my standard answer. 'It's not just their bottom I photograph, it's the confidence they find to show me their bottom.' Simple in words. Huge in impact. Would Apolline understand?

Whether she did or whether it was my price list, she finally found a smile somewhere. Guess I'd risen to 'right kind of people' status. 'Now I see how you can afford an assistant.'

'She pays me in kind.'

What a moment for Thibault to walk in! This time the bulging eyes were mine. I frantically shook my head at Apolline, shouting, 'Beau!'

'What? You haven't paid me anything yet. You've only given me a bed.'

'Separate! Separate beds. He lives...' I pointed up. 'And I...' My other arm crossed the first, pointing to my house. I must look crazy. Why did I even care what Apolline thought? But I did. Even if she didn't fancy a session, she might have rich friends I could convince.

Thibault shrugged. 'I don't think you'll be getting a letter about it now.'

What was his game?

Apolline lost the colour in her face, but Beau didn't seem to notice. He went on, 'What do you think? No more letters now that that woman has been killed?'

Apolline stammered some parts of words.

'What was in yours, anyway? I've heard some really funny ones.'

Apolline had devolved to no more than heavy breathing by this point.

Thibault still seemed oblivious. 'I wonder who will turn out to have done her in. Could be anyone, I reckon. Even you.' He gave her a sly grin, that somehow turned into his most charming smile, as if he hadn't all but accused her seconds ago.

'I've invited Marie Madora for a free shoot.' It was the only way I could think to save the situation. 'She was delighted with the offer.'

Apolline tore her gaze away from Beau and blinked a few times to get rid of the crazed element that had appeared in her eyes. 'Oh. Yes. I imagine that would be right up her alley. A much better way to appear in the limelight.' She tutted. 'I'm glad the Madoras found refuge here.'

Beau looked up. I was wondering the same thing: where did that come from? 'Refuge? From what?'

Apolline gave a demure smile. 'Oh, *ma chère*, that's not for me to say.' She straightened, throwing Thibault a vicious look.

'I think duty calls me next door. Thank you for the tour of your little studio, Julie. I'll be sure to recommend it to the right people.'

Oh, well, as long as they were the right people, then. I let Apolline out, ignoring Beau's humming of 'La Marseillaise' when I came back in.

'So, now we know I was right to suspect Madora,' he announced smugly.

'We also know, as we already knew, that she herself has a secret, as she was so quick to divert suspicion. But how are we going to find out about that now?' Crossing my arms, I raised an eyebrow at him.

Thibault shrugged. 'Don't ask me. I was getting there, but you had to butt in with Madora. I'm sure you'll think of something, though.'

'And have you found somewhere new to stay?'

'I'm sure I'll think of something.'

Before I could argue with that, Jacqueline came in through the glass front door of my studio, and Beau retreated upstairs, mumbling something about policewomen.

'I thought nothing ever happened in this village?'

'You're telling me. That's why I moved here.'

'Must be you, then.' She kissed both my cheeks now that she wasn't here in her professional capacity.

'All done up there?' I asked, pointing my thumb over my shoulder.

Eyes closed, Jacqueline sat down on the sofa, rubbing her temples with a sigh. 'Looks like she's done a runner.' She opened one eye. 'If Marc were here, he'd tell me that this was unofficial, but you'll hear it from him soon enough. Or from that woman who thinks she's all that.'

'Yes?' I sat in a chair but leaned forward. Not because I was curious, but to make her feel I was interested, you see.

'While we were looking in closets, the husband noticed some clothes and a suitcase missing. I don't think we'll be calling out a search party.'

Now that was interesting. 'She really left? Where would she go? She was pretty upset when I talked to her the day before yesterday.'

'Her mother? Usually the first one women think of, unless there's a kink in the relationship. But that didn't seem to be the case here. The husband didn't want to worry the mother, but when he did call, she said she'd had a text this morning. She thought that was a bit odd, but after all that happened, the mother was happy to have her daughter close.'

'Oh, so she was there already?'

'Not yet, but certainly not a matter for the police. This murder has everyone on tenterhooks.'

I nodded. 'I can add to that. You want to know what I found out?'

She opened one eye, clearly wondering if I could actually have uncovered something.

'Absolutely nothing. Next time you and *Maman* want me to socialise, throw me a party or something. This was at least as embarrassing.'

'Oh, you figured that out, huh? I'm sorry, but your mother was getting worried. And with the murder and all, we thought you'd stick your nose in anyway, so we might as well benefit from it.'

I took in an indignant breath. 'I would not! I never wanted anything to do with it.'

'Well, there you go. The old you certainly would have, before you moved here and started acting like a recluse.'

What?! 'I don't! I—'

'So nothing at all, huh. Did you at least come up with any theories?'

And now she was not even listening any more. How dare she want me to share my genius but not let me defend my actions. I should keep her in the dark and let her figure it all out by herself. Nothing to do with me. 'Well... everybody seems to have some kind of secret, or thing they don't want to talk about. Which is normal, right? The most logical course seems to be that La Mademoiselle – sorry, Claire Braymand – sent

out some really nasty letters, and someone else then sent a lot
more to avert suspicion.'

Both eyes opened now. 'You think the murderer sent out
most of the letters?'

'You said the poison was on the envelopes, but we all got
letters in self-adhesive envelopes. At least, Tiana and I did.
Nobody else wanted to admit to getting a letter.'

'Who did you talk to?'

'Marie Madora, Laurent Tariel, and Apolline Bailly.'

'Why them?'

'Marie and Apolline used to be Madame Braymand's
friends, before the post office closed, along with Mylène
Grasset and my mother, but Mylène only comes to the school
these days, and you'll forgive me for not suspecting my mother
of murder. She wouldn't know about that poison, anyway.'

Jacqueline straightened and held up one finger. 'Mind you,
that's not official yet. Toxicology reports take forever. Our
doc just happens to be a bit of a buff on plant-based poisons,
and this was his educated guess. Though we're pretty sure it
was plant-based poison, and it was definitely on the envelopes.
How the victim never noticed that greenish tint is beyond me,
but it sure helped us.'

'She had no reason to suspect foul play, I suppose. And
also, she was probably preoccupied, if she was sending more
of those vile letters.'

Jacqueline shrugged. 'But like I said, not official!'

'Then aren't you breaking some rule by telling me?'

'Yes.' Her dark gaze pierced mine. 'But I told you not to share that information. You didn't, did you?'

Ehm... 'Not really.'

She shot up. 'What?! Who did you tell?'

I felt my cheeks heat up. 'Just Beau and Tiana, and—'

'You told Thibault Fouquet?' She was fully into scary policewoman mode now.

'You said I could get him involved!'

'I said I was okay with him talking to the villagers. Not with you sharing police information with him. Have you forgotten what family he comes from?'

That, I knew all too well. And it was something I could defend myself on. 'They may be criminals, but killing an old lady in some village doesn't make sense, even for them.'

She groaned. 'That's it. You are relieved of duty. Let's hope I won't be. Just don't say anything about this to anyone until we find the killer, all right?'

'Fine! I didn't want to get involved in the first place.' How dare she get angry at me for something she herself dragged me into?

'I won't make that mistake again.' She made for the door. 'See you next Thursday?'

'Yes,' I said as I slammed the door behind her. Because we were friends. And we both knew that we'd been stupid. By Thursday we'd have calmed down, and we'd laugh again. Unless my telling the others would really get her fired. I tapped my chin as I thought about that.

Tiana would never tell a soul. Partly because she never spoke to a soul to begin with. Apart maybe from Lucas now, but I'd already told him, so that wouldn't be her doing. Lucas... I didn't know him at all. I'd trusted Ti's judgement, which was usually spot on, but Lucas had already shown a bit of a temper when Beau was joking around with him. He was probably the weakest link here, unless Beau...

My earlier doubts about Beau resurfaced. But then... I knew him. Didn't I? I couldn't be that wrong about him? That would mean that Lucas was still the most likely to blab, unless Tiana...?

I shook my head. No one would talk. I could trust them all, at least where the telling of police secrets was concerned, and Jacqueline would keep her job and find the killer. And if I happened to stumble upon a clue, she couldn't berate me for that, could she?

16

I'm sure we can think of something

Having just eaten breakfast, I wasn't very hungry, but if I didn't start preparing lunch now, I wouldn't have time to eat it before my client arrived. Of course, since I really wasn't hungry, I merely plonked on the couch that Jacqueline had just vacated, put on some Pat Boone, and started fiddling with my camera. As if on cue, Beau came in through the door from upstairs. No backpack. I clicked off a picture.

'Hm.'

'What?'

I knew that would get him curious. Most people are vain when it comes to their portrait, and the time he spent taming his blond mop told me he would be no different. 'Annoyingly, it's as I thought. The camera loves you.'

'Oh!' He grinned in relief. 'Yes, I know.'

Of course he did. 'That might work in your favour.'

'It usually does,' he answered breezily.

'I could agree to let you stay another night...'

That put his guard up. 'If...?'

'If you agree to a promo shoot. I could use more male clients.' Liar, liar, panties on fire. Though I occasionally had male clients, none of them would be won over by a picture of Thibault. The female clients, however... Letting him stay one more day couldn't hurt me, right? And it would absolutely help my business.

'I'm not showing you my buttocks! That's private.'

That's not what I'd heard. 'I'm sure we can... "think of something".' I wiggled my eyebrows.

Fists on hips, he threw me a nasty scowl. 'You're actually forcing me to take my clothes off? Against my will?'

'Nobody's forcing anything.' I held up my hands in defence. 'I'm certainly not forcing you to stay. But if you are, that's my condition.'

He kept silent, glaring at me.

'You're free to leave. But it's not some kind of sleazy deal! You know my work. It's peekaboo more than anything. You were more than happy to take your shirt off before.'

'I thought you'd have more sympathy.'

I might have had, if he hadn't shown up right when my ex-husband's scary best friend applied for a house in my village, and he hadn't had a meeting with the estate agent the previous night. He agreed to my terms, as I knew he would, but not as happily as I'd expected. I'd spent a good part of the previous night coming up with interesting poses for a male pin-up. Especially with one this pretty, it was supposed to be fun. But with him in victim mode, those pictures would not be usable to begin with. That was it, quick shoot in the morning, and he was out of here.

Maile arrived at ten to two, saying she couldn't stay later than three thirty because she had an errand to run for her mother-in-law. I shrugged. In emergencies, I could always fix hair and make-up myself. Especially after she'd laid her marvellous foundation. Maile disappeared to the dressing room, and I went to have a word with Beau. I found him polishing chrome.

'Just to let you know, the girl I'm shooting is under eighteen…'

He didn't even look up. 'You've already told me not to mess with your clients. What do you take me for?'

I wiggled my head, which I thought he couldn't see, but I hadn't counted on the reflective surface in front of him.

Now he looked up. 'Seriously? You don't think I can be professional, just because I happen to look good? You realise how discriminative you are, right?'

'I'm not going by looks alone here.' And now he had me defending myself. Not comfortable. He was so out of here.

'You don't know me that well, Julie.'

Not making me feel any better! If the arrival of my client hadn't called me away, I might have chucked him out there and then. Instead, I pasted on a smile and prepared to make someone happy.

Two girls, obviously sisters, came in through the glass door. Though they were from the village, I'd only met them both for the first time when they came for the preliminary consultation. The oldest, Justine, was a mild-mannered girl with a soft voice and a demure smile. Faustine, however, had the corners of her mouth almost perpetually turned down. She stared down on the world from a particularly high horse, expecting everyone to run to do her bidding. Unfortunately, it was Faustine I'd have in front of my camera today.

'Hello, girls, welcome.' I held my hand out to my office, where they both sat down. 'Before I leave you in the capable hands of Maile, let's go over the poses you selected once more.' I spread my cards out on the desk. 'These are good poses for you, so you'll look great. However, I do have an alternative, which I think you should consider instead of the swing. If you look through the window, you'll see a vintage Harley. Would you be interested in posing with that?'

Both girls stood and went to the window.

'Ooh, does he come with the bike? I want him to pose with me.'

I gave a fake chuckle. 'Unfortunately, Thibault is not part of any package I sell. But the bike I can include.'

'Can't I just ask him? I bet I can get him to pose with me.' Without waiting for an answer, she opened the window and leaned out, displaying her assets on the window sill. '*Coucou!* I'm going to be all over that bike of yours. Want to join me?'

I couldn't see Beau from behind my desk, nor hear his answer, but judging from the pout on Faustine's face, he'd firmly refused.

'All right, we'll start with Morning Concert, so I'll tell Maile to leave the rollers in.'

Leading them to the dressing room, I decided I'd stay as well. Normally I used the time the client took to get ready to go over my equipment, but since that was more for my own peace of mind than anything else – those checks had never revealed any fault at all – today might be a good time to deviate from my habit. I wanted to talk to these girls some more. They had grown up in the village and never left. They must have their own view on what had happened.

While Maile started working her magic, I made coffee.

'Thanks,' Faustine said when I placed her almond cappuccino on the dressing table. 'Good thing you came here. To the village, I mean. I was ready to die of boredom.'

Justine gave a soft tut.

'Oh, don't start. Not everyone's happy putting green stuff in brown stuff all day.'

'Our dad owns the nursery between Saint-Maurice and Pruniers,' Justine explained. 'We've been helping out since we were little.'

'And I'm so done with it.' She stretched the word 'so' almost to breaking point. The dramatic head roll that came with it forced Maile to take out a curler and start again. 'Two more months till my eighteenth birthday, and then I'm gone. Paris is calling. With drums and trumpets.'

'Oh, so this is a going-away present?' I asked.

Faustine snorted. '*Mais non!* He' – I assumed she meant her dad – 'has no idea I'm leaving. I had to practically beg him to let me do this. He thinks it's like a thank-you for helping out all those years, but with these pictures I'm sure to land me a cushy modelling job in the city of lights.'

Justine flashed me an apologetic smile. She seemed the kind of responsible young woman who would've already tried to convince her sister life wasn't always going to go her way, so I kept my thoughts to myself on that subject.

'Didn't you want to join your sister? You have the perfect mouth for it.'

Justine sucked in her plump lips and turned a delightful shade of pink. 'Oh... no, I... This is more to Faustine's taste.'

Maile had started on make-up, which kept Faustine from commenting on our conversation, but her hands flexed as if she was.

'I'm happy to keep "putting green stuff in brown stuff",' Justine continued. 'Paris does not call to me at all.'

'To be honest, this is the first time someone wants to use my pictures for anything other than the memory of the experience, and the pleasure of looking at them. But it does take most people a while to get used to the idea of having my kind of photo taken.'

'Not me. I'm ready to show the world what I've got.' Eyes closed, Faustine shimmied in her chair. Maile backed away, fake eyelashes fluttering to the ground. She picked them up and threw them away, but not before shooting me a look that spoke volumes. I made a face that said, 'Yes, I know. Not all of them have to be dragged out of their shell. Sometimes you get clients like this one, that you'd rather kick back into a shell'. At least, that's what I hoped she got from the face I made but straightened before Justine could see.

What Faustine had or didn't have would not show in my pictures. I did have some standards, believe it or not. Under eighteens got hot pants, no less. I wondered if she'd caught on to that or chose to ignore it the first five times I'd mentioned it.

'Looking gorgeous,' I said instead. 'Have you made plans for later? A face like that should be seen all over town.'

But all Faustine did was snort again. 'You mean Villefranche? Okay, maybe there's more than three young people there, so it's better than Saint-Maurice, but still.'

'You could go to Lyon,' I ventured, but Justine spoke up.

'There are plenty of young people here. You just think you're better than all of us.'

Danger, Will Robinson! A cat fight was hardly the atmosphere I was trying to create.

Faustine turned in her chair. 'Really? Because I'm the only one looking for some actual fun? Now that Constantin is gone, all that's left are the sleepy types.'

'Constantin? As in Constantin Bailly, Apolline's son?' He'd been a troublemaker, as far as I knew.

'Yeah.' Faustine grinned widely. 'He was fun. No wonder he rebelled against his goody-two-shoes parents. Do you know?' She leaned towards me. 'They think they're so bad because they go on these trips and bring back seeds they're not supposed to. They act like they're smuggling drugs or something. At least, that's what Constantin said.' She turned back to the mirror. 'I'm going to look him up when I'm in Paris. I bet he knows all the good places.'

'You're done,' Maile announced. 'Time to go pick out your clothes.'

'I want your bustier. It's sexy.'

I could see Maile swallow a remark, but only because I'd known her for so long. The girls didn't have a clue Maile wanted to say anything other than, 'I have a similar garment here.'

She pulled a white bustier dotted with red cherries off the rack.

'Those cherries are dumb. Don't you have *Playboy* bunnies or something? Or skulls?'

Biting my tongue, I took a baby doll nightdress off the rack. The floaty top layer was sheer enough to please Faustine, and the decent cover underneath was close enough to her skin colour that she might go along with it. 'Since you're starting with Morning Concert, you need night clothes.'

Faustine eyed the dress for two seconds, then shrugged. 'Cool.'

Several private eye rolls later, I'd managed to work Faustine into the top and satin knickers in a relatively decent fashion – that is, without half her anatomy almost falling out. The girl seemed determined to twist my style into something vulgar. Surprisingly, she was rather good at posing. She even took my direction well, so we had the first session nailed in no time. As soon as we were back in the dressing room, however, the diva side played up again.

'I don't do dresses.'

'That's fine – shorts will work just as well on the motorcycle. How about these denim ones?' I suggested, while Faustine was back in the chair, having the curlers removed. The pair I held in my hand was the skimpiest set I owned. If that didn't make her happy, I'd give up.

'Sure. But not the cherries.'

We settled on a short, light yellow Bardot top with underwires. Though it wasn't quite her colour, the main advantage was that she couldn't pull it down. Fixing the colour in post-production was a minor inconvenience in comparison. My usual encouragements felt insincere, though. Telling her she looked good, when she wasn't lacking in confidence to begin with, left a sour taste. I hoped it didn't shine through that my thoughts went in the opposite direction. Sometimes beauty really is only skin deep.

I took a deep breath. She was only seventeen. Perhaps her stint in Paris would teach her some humility. 'What's your plan when you go to Paris? Do you have somewhere to stay?' Where did that come from? She wasn't my responsibility.

We were on our way outside, when it hit me. I'd forgotten to set up my lights around the bike. I could punch myself! The one time I thought I'd be all right talking to my client instead of checking my gear. Ugh!

Unaware of my mental absence, Faustine nodded. 'Yeah, my *cousine* has an extra bed in her flat. She said I could stay as long as I help pay the rent. So I'll stay there for a couple of months until I get my own place.'

Right, right. Where had my softbox gone? 'That's nice.'

As I prepared to tell them they'd have to wait for me to set up, we entered the courtyard. Thibault was leaning against his bike, lighting already set up, almost perfectly. I felt my jaw drop, but there was nothing I could do about it. Adjusting the softbox, I mouthed my thanks, but he ignored me. Whether he was still annoyed, or anxious not to get the girls' fingerprints on his bike, I couldn't tell, as he had turned to help Faustine mount.

'Other right, *ma biche.*'

All right, apparently his doe and I were doing that pose first. Taking my camera out of the holster, I motioned her forward. 'Lean this way? Perfect. Eyes on me? That's beautiful. Chin down. Okay, now tip your pelvis... other way. No, I mean push your hips back.'

Faustine slid backwards on the saddle.

'I mean, kick out your booty.'

She still had her back arched.

Beau intervened. 'Stop sucking in your belly and show us your butt!'

As much colour as drained from my face showed up in Faustine's. I groaned inwardly. Bye-bye, reputation.

But then Faustine grinned. Her colour lightened to pink, and she dropped her belly onto the gas tank, sliding along in what she probably thought was a seductive move. It made for a good enough picture, but I was glad to see Beau turn away to talk to the demure sister.

We went through several more poses, but when I had Faustine come off the bike to pose against it, a cloud obscured the sun, and I needed my off-camera flash. I held it up to my left, but the light just wasn't right. I looked around for a stand or something, but before I could come up with a solution, Beau tutted, took the flash from my hand and held it up in exactly the right place.

Oh, he was going to get it later. I narrowed forewarning eyes at him, but again he ignored me. Excuse me? It was by my good graces he was even in here. So maybe my warning earlier had been a bit much, but I only had my client's best interest at heart. Okay, and maybe my reputation. But I'd fought hard for that too. I had a right to protect it.

After Thibault's remark, Faustine loosened up a little and seemed to enjoy her shoot more. She relaxed her overly sexy attitude, making the last pictures I took of her the best contenders for my wow shot. I worked my way through the rest of the shoot, trying to focus on my client and her experience, and not on my own emotions, but after two hours,

I was exhausted. When Céline came in with cupcakes and *Viennoiseries*, I almost sighed in relief.

Half an hour later, when we said goodbye to the girls, I was confident I would sell at least two or three of my pictures, despite my own feelings about the shoot. I made a giant mug of herbal tea and sank down on the sofa.

'Faustine is not the easiest of girls. She was in a good mood, though,' Céline said. Thibault had asked her to stay and made her tea, which she now sat sipping beside me.

Eyes closed, I leaned my head back against the couch, dreading what Beau would have to say.

He'd taken a beer from the fridge but hadn't said anything to me yet. 'She just needs more people to tell her no.'

Céline grinned. 'Ooh, look at you, *papa* Thibault. Didn't she fall for your charm?'

'She did, naturally.' He took a long pull on his beer.

'And?'

'And nothing. What's with this conviction that I can't control myself around girls? I have turned women down before, you know.'

'Oh, right, your principle.'

'Exactly. You don't need me, you don't get me.' He took another swig of beer and looked away, but I was almost sure the beer was to hide a smile.

I was glad Céline had unknowingly come to my aid, but I wondered why her attitude was so different from almost all other women I'd seen him with in the past days.

Céline seemed to guess my thoughts. 'I'm immune. We practically grew up together.'

'Known her since we were seven. Best summer camp ever.' Though he kept the conversation light, he avoided looking at me.

'Mmm. He proposed to me, there and then.' She fluttered her lashes at him, and he shrugged.

'Your loss.' He turned to me. 'Thanks for not making me pose with the witchy sister, Juju. I appreciate that.'

Oh! That was unexpected. 'Hadn't even crossed my mind. I would never force you to pose. Well, except tomorrow, when I shoot you before I kick you out.'

The reminder of our previous conversation only caused a tiny stiffening of his lips. His light-hearted response was mostly for Céline's benefit, I expected. 'You still haven't realised how much you need me?'

''Fraid not.'

'I'm useful. I can cook your *déjeuner*.' Now why did that remind me of the garlic I saw him crush with his palm? Though I tried to hide my slight flinch, his eyebrow raised ever so slightly, but he didn't comment. 'I could fold your laundry.'

I almost spat out my tea. 'No! No, thank you.'

'What? I know my way around ladies' undies.'

'I'm sure. But not mine, and we're going to keep it that way.'

Céline snorted. 'Strike one, Thibault. Where will you go, if you can't stay here?'

'Well, I do know one other person in Saint-Maurice.' He wiggled his eyebrows.

That's right. Another person he could have asked to stay with instead of with me. But then, she lived with her father, and she was quite a sensible girl.

'Ha! You're not sleeping in my bed. I'll put the tent up for you.'

'It's October! You heartless creature.' He poked her in the side, making her giggle.

Before I could start to feel really old, I changed tactics. 'Thank *you* for setting up the scene. It completely slipped my mind, and I don't think the witchy sister, as you called her, would have appreciated the wait.'

Beau nodded in acknowledgement, but Céline made a face.

'It's not nice to call her a witch. She's just a little spoilt.'

'Very spoilt,' Beau corrected.

'Most of my clients need a bit of a confidence boost, but she has it in spades.' I shrugged. 'I've had them before, though, clients you need to slow down instead.' That's why I don't do boudoir. Too much emphasis on the sexy and not enough on the sass. 'Faustine took the pampering for granted, but her sister was gracious.'

'Justine is such a nice girl. We've been friends for ages. She knows everything about the plants her father grows. She also has amazing plans for the business once he lets her in. You know, once they've recovered.'

'What do you mean? What happened?' I asked.

She hesitated. 'Oh, you don't know? I'm not sure I should say... A lot of it is gossip.'

'Come on, you can't leave us hanging,' Beau said.

'Okay... well... I suppose it's not *my* gossip...' She took a breath. 'You know all the letters that have been going around?'

Both Thibault and I nodded. Obviously we were aware.

'A troll with an old-fashioned streak, if you ask me,' Beau said.

'According to Justine, her family didn't get one, and Faustine felt left out, so she made her own. Something about her dad scamming clients. She then showed it to anyone who'd listen, for a laugh. But some people believed it, and the business took a big hit. Justine says her dad wasn't even angry with Faustine, but with the person writing all the poison pen letters in the first place.'

Beau leaned back in his chair, extending his hand to me. 'There, another suspect for your inquiry into La Mademoiselle's murder.'

'It's not *my* inquiry,' I bit back.

Céline's eyes widened. 'You think Madame Braymand sent those letters?'

I held up my palms, trying to come up with a nuanced answer, but Beau steamed ahead.

'Not all of them. Probably not any of the ones we've seen or heard about. We think she only sent out letters to people who really have secrets they want to keep secret. But the person who murdered her sent out fake letters to many more people, to divert suspicion.'

'Except everyone without a letter would immediately be suspicious.'

'That's what I said,' I agreed.

Céline looked puzzled. 'But we know everyone. What would people have to hide?'

I almost laughed at her innocence. 'Illegally imported seeds, for one. Though I agree with Faustine, that doesn't seem the highly criminal act worth killing for. Then again, you never know.' I filled them in on Faustine's scoff about Apolline and Corentin Bailly and their cactus collection. 'But there are plenty of things people could want to hide from others. If we're right about La Mademoiselle, she'd want to hide the fact that she sent out poison pen letters.'

'Yes, but that's an exception.'

'Okay,' Thibault said, 'how about love affairs? Shady deals? Addictions?'

In shock, she grabbed his arm. 'We don't have those!'

'But if you did, who'd be the most likely person to know about it?'

She thought about that. 'I suppose it could be the person sorting everyone's post... But that information would be years old.'

I held up my palms. 'It could still be relevant. If you had an affair ten years ago, would you want your husband to know about it now?'

More shock. 'I would never!'

'Julie, you're scaring our baby,' Beau mock-admonished me, back to avoiding looking at me. 'I think she needs an ice cream.' He stood. 'Are you coming?'

I wondered if Céline picked up on the atmosphere between us, since to me the air itself seemed to turn frigid. I really needed to talk to him about all this, but I didn't want to bother Céline with it. That was when my phone rang. I motioned for the kids to go ahead and tapped my screen. 'Hi *Maman*.'

'What did you say to her?'

'To whom?' As if I didn't know.

'Apolline Bailly! She phoned me just now with a confusing story about Madame Durand missing, and your assistant accusing her of murder. She pretty much wants him banned from the village.'

I barely held back a giggle. 'I know how she feels.'

'This is not a joke, Julie.'

'You were the one who set me up to talk to people. Now I'm talking, and you want me to stop.'

'I wanted you to talk to the right people.'

'You sound like Apolline.'

My mother tutted. 'I wanted you to make some friends. All you do is work and sulk.'

'I don't sulk.'

'Then what are you doing when you're not working?'

For a second, that made no sense. Then I realised I was always working. Before Thibault arrived, I hadn't had a conversation in a long time that didn't involve some aspect of work, mine or someone else's, including my mother's. Although she did sometimes talk about family I wasn't in contact with any more. Even talking to Tiana usually came down to work successes or work troubles for either of us.

'In any case, I don't want you talking to Apolline if you're going to treat her as a suspect. You're off the case.'

'You've seen too many police dramas, *Maman*.' Although Jacqueline had said something very similar. But when your mother says it, it's not the same. When your mother says it, you either feel guilty or rebellious. And I did not feel guilty.

'Oh, and one more thing. She wanted me to invite you to next week's council meeting.'

That time I really did snort.

'It's not such a strange request. You are a part of the community now, and you can have your say.'

'She saw my price list, that's all. I've been promoted to Potentially Right Person because I make a lot of money.'

'And if that's all you do, there's all the more reason for you to broaden your horizon. The council meeting is not the worst place to start. I'll expect you next Tuesday at seven. Bring a snack to share.'

And with that, she hung up. I stared at my phone screen. My mother wasn't usually this curt. I must have hit her where it hurt somehow. Maybe, deep down, she knew her local hero wasn't as perfect as she wanted her to be. But, truth be told, I couldn't make myself care right now. This blip would be forgotten as soon as I had a normal conversation with my mother next time I saw her. And what Apolline did or didn't do was entirely up to her. I'd make sure I'd have another appointment Tuesday night.

I ate dinner by myself. It was almost strange not to share a meal. I made an effort to enjoy the quiet and my own thoughts, but I kept hearing Thibault's voice, teasing me into investigating. Like he did before we fell out. I still wasn't sure whether he was actually angry with me or had somehow picked up on the doubts I had about him. But I much preferred the situation before, when he was nice and in my way, instead of grumpy and in my way. Now that not even Beau wanted me to stick my nose in any more, though, I found myself still wondering who could have means, motive, and opportunity. Had they been right about pushing me towards this? I huffed. No doubt it was their pushing that had awakened this curiosity. Nevertheless, curious I was.

Beau was convinced the killer had had a different letter from the ones we'd seen. But what if that wasn't the case? There wasn't any evidence for two sets of letters. And since some people had had their letters after La Mademoiselle died, that would mean that she didn't send them in the first place. But who else? And if she hadn't sent the letters, why would anyone murder her?

I swallowed. If she hadn't sent the letters, would the reason to kill her be enough to kill me? The similarities I'd seen before loomed even larger: a woman alone in a village where she used to belong, but now lived as a strange entity in a friendless bubble. Both our houses were located at the edge of the village, albeit on opposite sides. Little enclaves of solitude. Sure, I did still have a few friends, but there had been moments where I felt like shouting at someone who would veer into my driveway without obvious cause, 'Go away!' Not at the children selling lily of the valley on the first of May, obviously, like La Mademoiselle had done. For me, it was mostly men. Only men, if I was being honest. In fact, I had been poised to shout it at Thibault when he pulled up, but the shock of recognition had shrivelled the words in my throat. Was writing poison pen letters the next step? Or were the two instances completely unrelated after all?

Of course, Apolline had let on that she'd had a letter she suspected was written by La Mademoiselle, but had she really? Maybe she was cleverer than she acted, casting suspicion away from herself.

I picked up my plate and started on the dishes. Who else was there? Marie Madora, according to Apolline, carried a real secret around. But how we were supposed to find out what that was...

I would have written off Laurent Tariel, if not for his meeting with Thibault. He'd admitted going to Claire Braymand's house, but his motives were supported by, yet again, Apolline. That might have been the end of that, but then why had he given Beau that little something yesterday evening?

Then there was Mylène Grasset. If she came to the Madora house to drop off a left *doudou*, then she could easily have passed by La Mademoiselle's house one day without anyone noticing. But if she never talked to her any more, why would she? What could be her motive? The fact that La Mademoiselle was yelling at children couldn't be enough to kill her?

And now we also had Faustine and Justine's father. But as Faustine had written her letter herself, her dad couldn't possibly know who had sent the originals, right? Could we really add him to our list of suspects?

Lucas? Did I really want to go there?

As for means and opportunity, any of the people on my list had abundant knowledge of plants. Finding a couple of poisonous ones shouldn't be too difficult. Most of them said they hadn't been to Claire Braymand's house, or at least not in the past few years. But who was to say those envelopes hadn't been there for a long time? Would any killer wait that patiently for that long, though? Laura Durand and Laurent Tariel were the only ones who had been inside Madame Braymand's house lately. But then something hit me. How did Marie Madora know that Laurent Tariel had been to visit La Mademoiselle? Her house was down in the valley, and the whole *quartier* of Moulin would obstruct her view of Claire Braymand's house.

My phone buzzed, displaying Marie Madora's name. I dried my hands and picked up, wishing I'd had more time to process that thought. But maybe I could ask her about it.

'*Oui*, Marie?'

'Hi Julie. I, erm...' She paused, revealing what she was going to say.

'You'd like to book that free shoot?'

'Yes.' Relief blew through the line.

'Great! Would you have time tomorrow morning?' Before she ran out of courage. If she agreed, perhaps I could find a sneaky way to bring up the Tariel matter. Also, it was a shoot I was giving away, thanks to Beau. He might as well make himself useful while he was here.

'Oh. Erm... all right.'

We made an appointment for ten o'clock. The way this was going, I was going to run out of time for editing my last shoots. I had a reveal coming up on Monday, but fortunately I'd finished all the work for that. If nothing else came up, I could just fit in a shoot with Marie in the morning, and one with Beau in the afternoon, but I'd need to do some editing straight after if I wanted to keep my Sunday free. And my work-free Sundays were sacred. At least with Beau out of the way, he wouldn't distract me any more by then.

I shot off a text to ask Maile if she had time the following morning, which came back positive almost immediately. Retreating to my office to schedule some social media posts, I worked until I heard the Harley start up around ten. It then woke me up at three, since my bedroom is on the courtyard side. Grumbling, I went back to sleep. Big day tomorrow. No more Harley.

17

Your heroine needs coffee

Thibault was in trouble next time Tiana saw him. Ever since he'd jokingly accused Lucas of... What had he accused him of? It hadn't felt like anything but a joke, but Lucas had taken it badly. Tiana hadn't heard from him all day yesterday. She shouldn't be surprised. Today was Saturday, they'd only met four days ago. They'd spent a great day together, although it ended weirdly. So what did she expect? He hadn't even kissed her. Well, he'd kissed her hand, but that didn't count. Not in this century.

She stared at her screen. Her heroine was bawling her eyes out over the love of her life, who'd left her. If she went on like that, she'd be deleted. No one wants a weak heroine.

Tiana pushed away from her computer. She'd gone straight to writing after her shower, skipping breakfast. Did she have any crisps? Or biscuits? Oh right, she'd taken them over to Catherine. No, wait, she'd taken an empty plate back to

Catherine. That's when the whole thing had started. *Oh, not him again! Get out of my head!*

She needed a biscuit. Julie would have biscuits, but she sometimes had clients on Saturday. Maybe Catherine would take pity on her. Lucas was supposed to finish up there yesterday, so there would be no risk of running into him. Switching off her computer, Tiana grabbed her phone and trudged next door.

'*Bonjour, ma petite!* You look depressed.'

Had she sunk to that level already? 'My heroine is a wuss.'

'Your heroine needs coffee. Here.'

Chocolate biscuits. How did Catherine know every time? Tiana sat and dunked and drank, while Catherine sipped her own coffee, patiently waiting for once.

'It's silly, really,' Tiana began.

Catherine shook her head. 'That's what we all think we should be saying, but what we really want to do is scream. Maybe you should. Go on, scream.'

Smiling, Tiana shook her head.

'Sure! You'll feel better. Okay, I'll scream with you. You know what? I'll start.' She let out a bellow that echoed around the kitchen. 'WAAAH! WHY HAS THAT GORGEOUS MAN NOT RETURNED MY CALLS? WE WERE SO GOOD TOGETHER AND NOW HE'S IGNORING ME!'

Banzaï jumped up and scarpered. Hands over her ears, Tiana chuckled.

'Am I right?' Catherine asked in her normal voice.

'I suppose my story isn't very unique.'

Catherine held up her hands. 'Everyone's story is both common and unique.'

'Is everything all right?' Daniel came into the kitchen, using his I-don't-expect-trouble-but-just-in-case voice.

'We were just screaming at Lucas.'

'*You* were screaming,' corrected Tiana.

'But he's not here. Oh, is that why you were screaming?'

Catherine stroked his cheek. 'No, *mon amour*. We were screaming because he's being a man.'

'Ah.' Daniel picked up a newspaper and sat down at the kitchen counter.

Catherine turned back to Tiana. 'So he didn't show his face yesterday? How about the day before?'

Feeling her anxiety ebb away, Tiana clutched her coffee in both hands. 'Well, he asked if I had plans for Thursday, which, of course, other than writing, I hadn't. So he came round on Thursday morning, and we...' She sighed. 'I don't even remember what we did. Just walked around, talking. But I've never talked to anyone so easily before. He was interested in my stories and why I write them. Really interested, you know? Not just the "Oh, you're a writer, how interesting", but asking about my characters and why they do what they do. But then Beau said something about the murder—'

'Who's Beau?'

'Thibault, Julie's new assistant.'

Catherine clapped her hand over her ample bosom. 'New blood! What fun. What's he like? No, finish your story first.'

With a little smile, Tiana continued, 'Well, he said that they were trying to find the murderer, and that it could even be Lucas, or something like that, and he got angry. We all knew it was a joke, but he started defending himself. When it was just us again, he got back to normal. That is, until we were saying goodbye, and all of a sudden he acted all weird, but in a different way. He said he had fun, but he never reacted to my texts yesterday.'

'You didn't bombard him, did you?'

Frowning, Tiana pulled away. 'I write romance, give me some credit.' She hesitated. 'I did mention Happily Ever Afters, but he was asking about my books, so...'

'So...' Catherine's eyes sparkled. 'Did he kiss you?'

'No!' Tiana almost wailed it. 'I got a hand kiss, for crying out loud.'

A rare thing happened. Catherine sat quietly for a moment, staring at Tiana's face. 'He didn't say much when he finished the work yesterday. I thought that was because he wanted to get back to you, so I didn't push him to talk, but now I see. The way he wound you around his little finger… I *thought* he would be trouble. Didn't I say so, *mon amour*? These Americans, can't trust them.'

Since Daniel didn't look up, Tiana answered instead. For some reason, she felt the need to defend Lucas. 'I'm not perfect either, you know. I sometimes nuke my tea.'

Catherine feigned shock. 'Careful who you say that to. Good thing I'm not British.'

'I know, I'm a monster. But I live in a really cold house, so I have about a five second window to drink my tea when it goes from too steaming hot to too cold for comfort. And since I, like any self-respecting writer, spend most of my time dreaming, that five second window is just far too small. It's not like I heat up day-old tea. I claim extenuating circumstances.'

Laughing together felt good, and Tiana was glad she'd come down to talk to her neighbours.

Even Daniel looked up with a grin. 'I think he just had an off day yesterday. When I was walking Banzaï, I passed him outside the cemetery. He was sitting in his car, shaking a sheet of paper and talking on the phone. Rather loudly, I must say. Didn't seem very happy. But he's well respected around the school. The other governors and I regularly get to commend him on excellent work. I'm sure you'll hear from him soon.'

It was meant to reassure her, but as she returned home, it did exactly the opposite. So Lucas was having fun with the school kids, but she wasn't important enough? She shook her head to the hall mirror when she came back home. That wasn't fair, was it. Entering her living room, she tripped over a shoe box. Grr, those boots! She'd put the box by the door, ready to be brought back to where they belonged, but Laura still hadn't returned her text.

Who needs men, anyway? Before you know it, you're hiding boots from them. Maybe she was better off without a grouch like that, if he couldn't see the humour of Thibault's accusation. She grimaced. That wasn't fair either. She stopped in her tracks, eyes the size of saucers. What if he'd read one of her books, and that's why he didn't react? Hand over her mouth, she lowered herself onto a chair. What if it was *Not Now, Not Ever*? If he hadn't made it all the way to the end... Or *Bite Me*? She sucked her bottom lip between her teeth. Oh no, what if he'd read *No Way No How*? Even if he had read it through, that one was ambiguous at best. Not her most popular work. Maybe she should send him *All the Way* instead? Just to be sure? Burying her face in her hands, Tiana groaned. No way no how was she writing anything romantic today.

18

We can grill her without her noticing

After breakfast – another meal by myself; was my life going back to normal? – I opened the front door to my younger brother, David. Not normal then. I usually only saw him at *Maman*'s, since he was either busy working or seeing friends in town.

'Something wrong?'

'Good morning to you too. Any chance of a cup of coffee?'

'I'll have one too, please.' Beau sauntered into the kitchen, fresh as a... Hm, no, daisy did not suit him, and I couldn't think of a manly yellow flower. But he looked remarkably well rested for someone who'd only come in at three. He took two mugs from the cupboard, filled them, and planted one on the kitchen table in front of my brother, who seemed lost for words at the appearance of a handsome young man in my house.

'Who are you?'

'Thibault. Who are you?'

Before a cock fight could break out, I put the sugar on the table. Introductions were in order. 'Thibault, my very temporary assistant. David, my brother. The one who lives in La Grande Maison.'

'The Big House? Very creatively named.'

David straightened. 'That's not what it's called. It's what it's known as. Has been for several hundreds of years.'

If they hadn't been in my kitchen, I'd have found this instant dislike extremely funny. If only I'd had my camera. My brother's hair, a few shades darker than mine, was almost black. The way they were facing off, they could be movie star opponents in a comedy. But in this setting, I was worried for my crockery.

'So you're *le choix du roi*, aren't you? Prince David and princess—'

'Don't you start!' I'd had to listen to this all my life. 'He's not the heir to the throne, and I have no desire to be married off, thank you very much. Now drink your coffee and behave. David, what do you want?'

His smirk turned in my direction and vanished. '*Maman* said you'd had one of these as well?'

He produced a simple, white, self-adhesive envelope and held it out to me. The letter inside made no sense at all.

'Why would you play fast and loose with your nurses? They're so far beneath you.'

'Exactl— No! Contrary to popular belief, I appreciate "my" nurses very much, but not in the way that letter says. What was in yours?'

'I know about your husband.'

David waited for more, then said, 'That's it?'

I shrugged.

'At least that's not an outright lie.'

'When did you get it?' Beau asked.

David shrugged one shoulder. 'This morning. Or maybe last night. It wasn't there when I looked in the mailbox yesterday morning.' They seemed to have forgotten their dislike in the face of this bit of mystery.

Beau looked at me. 'So they're still sending them.'

I nodded slowly. 'Seems a bit desperate, though. As far as I know, the other letters at least had some truth in them. I mean, there's no...?' I pulled up my eyebrows at my brother.

'Absolutely not!'

'Just checking.'

Beau grinned behind his mug, which David didn't notice, fortunately.

Emptying his cup, my brother got up. 'Better get to work. Some of us have important things to do. We can't all choose our own hours.'

'That's right. Some of us are smart,' I retorted.

'Have fun looking at bums all day.'

'Isn't that exactly what you do? At least mine are healthy.'

He was already halfway through the door, when he turned. 'I'm off skiing in a few weeks, but I hear I'll see you at the council meeting on Tuesday?'

Ugh! 'No, I... have... a thing.' Crap.

Smirk was back. 'See you on Tuesday.'

I slammed the door behind him.

'Stuck-up much?' Beau was at the kitchen window, sipping from his mug.

'Hm. I try to prevent God-complex as often as I see him, but that hasn't made our relationship much better.'

Putting his mug in the sink, he opened his arms wide. 'Where do you want me?'

I almost choked. 'Excuse me?'

'I checked your calendar. You have no clients today, so I'm ready for my shoot.'

'Oh!' A relieved chuckle came out at an only slightly crazy pitch. 'Actually, Marie Madora called me last night, so we're doing her first.' Which meant I'd have to postpone our talk yet again. On the one hand, I dreaded it. Thibault now acted like nothing had ever been wrong between us, and I really wanted to talk to him about my realisation that Marie Madora couldn't have known about Laurent Tariel visiting La Mademoiselle. On the other, he could be in league with Tariel, so did I really want to share my insight with him? No time to think about it now, since a mother-of-pearl Mini drove up. 'Here's Maile now.'

My make-up artist's heels clicked on the pavement of my driveway.

Beau looked a little deflated. 'So I could have stayed in bed?'

'No, you're supposed to be my assistant. Assist.'

'Can I take some of the pictures?'

'No, that would make you the photographer. And that role is taken.' I'll never know why I added, 'But if you're interested, I could show you later?'

One corner of his mouth lifted as he considered my proposal. 'Yeah, I'd like that.'

Oh, joy. Why had I said that? Now I not only had to direct him but explain what I was doing in the meantime. At least he already knew about composition and lighting from his drawing. It might not be fun, exactly, but it could be good for my position in The Talk that I was dreading more and more. Maybe he'd asked as a kind of peace offering. He seemed to have put his indignation behind him. Then again, he didn't know I'd spied on his little rendez-vous with Laurent Tariel. But as I followed him out of the kitchen, I plucked my negativity from my brain and left it by the door. I'd never shared my professional knowledge before. If only as a bit of personal and professional growth, teaching him would do more good than harm. Probably.

Feeling that my brain must have predicted it might actually be fun or I wouldn't have suggested it in the first place, I trotted across the courtyard, just in time to let a slightly hunched Marie Madora into my studio. We would have to combine the preliminary consultation with the shoot. For one because she'd already made the appointment. And for two because she wasn't paying, so I'd better make this quick. But boy, was she nervous. She'd caked on the make-up extra thickly, hiding her eyes behind giant movie star sunglasses.

Thibault startled me when he whispered in my ear, 'Very smart. Invite the main suspect so we can grill her without her noticing.'

'She is not our main suspect,' I hissed. 'We have no main suspect. Now go get me two cappuccinos.'

I let Marie Madora into my office with the most genuine smile I could conjure up. She was here, apparently in spite of herself. She needed me to be here for her, which conflicted me. Photographer me saw the woman who needed my help. But that little bit of curious me, who just had to get involved, albeit through someone else's intervention, made me wary of the fact that this woman-who-needed-me might just be a cold-hearted killer.

Add to that the fact that the past few days I had been pushed into doing things that I hadn't chosen to do, and you can imagine my unwillingness to do this free shoot. It wasn't the money. More that I was being paid with information I hadn't sought out in the first place. Thibault and his great ideas...

However, if I could make Marie feel at ease, that would be a feather in the cap of my business's mission statement. Looking at her, I wasn't sure making this client feel confident and beautiful wouldn't require a miracle, but who knew? Maybe sainthood was in my future.

'I'm so glad you decided to accept my offer.' Beau's offer, but, you know...

She gave me a small smile. 'I'm still a little nervous.'

'Don't worry, most women are. Why don't you have a look at some of my poses and see if anything calls to you?' Placing the album in front of her, I wondered which of the poses would actually work for her, since she only had the use of one arm. I'd never done a shoot like that before. While she leafed through my album, I tried to work out how to adapt any pose she paused at, babbling in the meantime about coming back to Saint-Maurice and hoping it wouldn't be too far out in the country to attract new clients, but that until now everyone had raved about the location. It made most people feel relaxed to be out in the country, no eyes on them but mine. But Marie must be used to the surroundings?

'I am, mostly. But I make it a point to stand still and enjoy the view at least once a week. If you lose appreciation for the little things, you're not worth the big ones.'

Despite the dark glasses, I could see her eyes never left my pictures when she said that. Nothing about her said 'killer'. Of course, according to Beau, it was her husband who had done it, but what connection did he have with La Mademoiselle?

'I'm with you on that. We're lucky to live in such a picturesque place.'

Marie sniggered at Wet Behind the Ears, where the skirt was up after falling in the little stream at the end of my garden.

'If you like that one, the weather today should be warm enough for it. I could even offer you a poolside shoot, if you'd like.'

She quickly turned the page. 'No, thank you.'

Was it me, or had a cloud passed over her face?

'Or, if you like, I have a vintage Harley you could pose with?'

She gave a modest chuckle. 'Do I look like the fast type?'

'I don't know. What does the fast type look like?'

'Well... not like me. I'm more the last type.'

I frowned at my album. 'What do you mean?'

'Oh, just... last in line, you know?'

Ahhh. That I did know. At least from many of my other clients. 'That's actually very common. As soon as we have kids, family comes first.'

She looked up, then nodded.

'But you know what?' I reached across the desk and laid my hand over hers. 'You're here now. This is all about you. You get to pick what you want to do, and we'll make sure you look gorgeous doing it.' I let that sink in. Marie's eyes flicked to the album on the desk. Swallowing my pride, I added, 'And if you don't feel comfortable enough with your bum in the air, we'll find a more demure pose.'

'No!'

It came out so vehemently that it startled me.

'You're right, this is about me. I'll take With Sprinkles and Too Hot to Handle, please.' She took a deep breath and let it go with the biggest relieved smile. Then she took off her glasses.

'All right! Let's do this!'

She looked so happy, that it made me laugh, which in turn made her laugh. Confidence? Check. Beauty? Check. Sainthood, here I come. This day had just got a whole lot better.

Maile had taken my sainthood away. The miracle was entirely hers. After checking my equipment and informing Thibault which poses we were doing, I walked into an unrecognisable Marie Madora in the dressing room. She looked at least ten years younger with the new make-up, and the airy green dress accentuated all the right curves. But it wasn't even the outside that had changed the most. Marie stood straight, shoulders back, chin up, eyes wide open and gleaming.

'Let's go!' she almost shouted. 'I'm ready to moon the world.'

Still a bit nervous, then. But also excited now. I grinned. 'Let's get you set up.'

If I took my time posing her, she'd settle into a comfortable confidence. Even if it fell away back in normal life, I'd had former clients tell me that they derived strength just from looking at their portraits and reliving those moments in their minds. I hoped it would do the same for Marie.

'Okay, what I'd like you to do... put your hand—' No, if she put her hand on the tap, she'd be facing away from the camera. While I was still working things out in my head, Marie had switched on the tap and was flapping her skirt around in the shower of the garden sprinkler system, laughing and jumping up and down. I'd have to work quickly if I didn't want her to be soaked in all the photos. The first few were lovely pictures of Marie having fun, but this was not my brand at all. 'That's fine, doing great. Now try to act surprised. Bend over as far as you can with straight legs. Beautiful. Thibault? I'm going to need that scrim. Higher, please.'

The edge of the screen used to diffuse direct sunlight still cast a shadow. Beau stretched, turned, hopped back and forth and generally made a spectacle of himself. I was about to get annoyed when I realised that, once again, he'd calmed my client down. Marie had gone from overexcited to enjoying herself, and when I posed her, she did what I asked and got herself some stunning pictures. No barring shadow in sight.

'You're a natural,' I said. 'Have you modelled before?'

A tinkling laugh worthy of Snow White sounded. 'No, but thanks. Maybe after this, I'll consider it.'

'Chin down. Would it please the boys?'

'As long as I'd still always be there for them. Like you said, family comes first.'

'Lean towards me a little? Hand a bit higher. Perfect.' Click. 'You must have things you enjoy doing just for you, though? Gardening? Baking?' The poses my clients pick usually say a lot about their personality.

Marie's face went into the perfect surprised face I needed for my picture. Click. 'How did you know? Yes, those are the things I spend most of my time on.'

So the botanic knowledge was there. That took care of means. Opportunity could be years old, so all I needed now was motive. I slid my camera into the holster on my hip. 'Time for your next outfit. Maybe you should trade secrets with Céline. The baker's daughter? Her cupcakes are divine. Or maybe you go foraging with Apolline?'

She gave me a puzzled look as we retreated back inside. 'Apolline? Why?'

'She told me she likes to collect nature's prizes or something. And she had something in the oven when I visited.'

'Oh! Haha, well, it is Apolline.' I thought she was going to leave it with that mysterious statement, but after a few seconds, she continued, 'No, foraging on Apolline's knowledge wouldn't get you very far. But she does like to cook. How about you, what do you do?'

I wiggled my camera in answer while she unzipped her dress.

'That can't be all you do?'

Maile gave me the side-eye as she handed my client a purple skirt and a lacy white blouse. 'Oh, it is.'

'Really?' Marie said from inside the skirt she was working over her head. 'That's it, you're coming with me on my next walk. You do have something other than heels, don't you?'

'I... do.'

Emerging from the skirt, Marie gave me a motherly frown. 'Ballet flats don't count. We'll go get you some good shoes, and I'll take you walking. Consider it payment for' – she spread her arms – 'all this.'

My first reaction was to refuse, but hadn't I missed walking around the countryside? Then I wanted to refuse because she could be a murderer. Not that she'd given me any indication that she might be. Her invitation had me torn, but she was waiting for an answer, so I accepted. I could do with a new friend, if only to put more psychological distance between me and La Mademoiselle. And I liked Marie.

With a new hairstyle, Marie followed me through to the mock kitchen I had installed in the studio just for posing purposes. Beau had already had his comment about it at least being the size of a real kitchen, of course, but this one I kept gleaming. None of the appliances were connected. My gaze fell on the biscuit tin. Since I hadn't had any more of the cookies I'd baked, I wondered if they would have gone by now, like the other ones before. I couldn't resist a peek... huh. Real cookies. I wouldn't have to use the plastic ones today. Maybe Beau hadn't been hungry at three o'clock in the morning.

I turned around to find Thibault's smirk in my face. 'Don't eat them all *before* the shoot, Juju.'

Out, you cookie-stealing, estate-agent-dealing, semi-criminal ex-nephew. Pushing past him, I opened the oven door and took out the cookie sheet, dumping all the plastic cookies in an empty drawer. While I filled the sheet with the real cookies, Marie settled on the couch, giving me the usual chitchat about how she loved my style but would never have considered it if not for – insert whatever reason here. Usually it was someone else gifting my experience cards. In Marie's case, of course, I'd invited her myself. Or Thibault did, sort of.

But as the shoot progressed, so did the conversation. She told me about her life before kids, when she and Maarten had lived in the Netherlands. They'd made a fortune in inflatable water slides and had travelled all over the world.

'Me, I'm more of a couch traveller. See the world on the TV screen,' I admitted. 'Don't tell anyone, though. With my' – I coughed – 'sophisticated subjects, they expect me to be a citizen of the world. I suppose there is a free-spiritedness about it that speaks to people's imaginations. You'd think that's what would have been in one of those letters that are going around.'

'But it wasn't?' The question sounded innocent enough. I'd hoped this would be my in to find out about her letter. Maybe I should push just a little further.

'No. It... was about my ex-husband, who's in jail.' Everyone knew about him. Then why was it still not easy to say?

'Oh.'

And apparently I'd shared that bit of information for no good reason. I brought up the camera and posed Marie for another shot. Her heart wasn't in it, though, and I couldn't get the expression right. I shouldn't have brought up the letters. She wasn't going to share, and now she was distracted. Maybe I could save myself with some more chitchat.

'So how come you settled in France?'

I'd expected a dreamy reaction on France being the place where everything came together, but instead she straightened from the bent-over position I'd posed her in, and I had to put the camera down. Her hands fluttered up and down while restless eyes scanned the room. When she finally looked my way, her eyes glazed over.

'There was... an incident. With one of our slides. Though we were never officially blamed, people talked, and it killed our reputation, as well as our... Well, everything went to the sharks. It was... not a good time. We had to sell the business and decided to start over in a different place.' She seemed to shake off her blues then and smiled. 'We found this wonderful village where we could live off the money from the sale, so that's what we did. And when the kids came, well... I haven't looked back since. But doing this... It's different. I think I've been a mum for so long that I've forgotten to do things just for me.' She looked me straight in the eye. 'Thank you.'

Smiling, I raised my camera and clicked off a picture of her radiance. Beautiful.

'Beau, can you hold that reflector a little higher? Little higher?' He stretched his pretty form out all the way, the light bouncing in a ridiculous angle. By the look on his face, he knew very well that I was trying to get back at him for his cookie remark. The look also said that he wasn't going to take the bait. 'Okay, lower, please.'

The last picture caught Marie looking light as a feather, and I promised her I'd have her pictures within the week.

'If you're still around.'

We both stared at Beau with a worried expression. Marie's worry was probably whether he was mentally okay, but my worry was whether that was a threat.

'Well, you know, with people getting murdered around here.'

'Thibault, that's—' I started, but Marie's worry had turned to sympathy.

'I know. Scary, isn't it? Someone so... Hm. I went to see her a few weeks ago. At least I wanted to because I felt sorry for her. But then... I couldn't. It's a shame. You know, she used to be my friend. She knew... everything... about me. But I just... couldn't. I wanted to try again, but now it's too late. It's all so senseless, isn't it? Makes you wonder. I can see why you're worried, Thibault, but I don't think you have to be. You can't stop living because you're scared of death.'

She put her hand on his arm with an encouraging smile, and he played along with the same utterly convincing charm that threw me every time I was reminded of how easily he could be using it on me. But Marie had no clue. She was still glowing from her experience and gushed over her plans to talk to her boys about what a wonderful morning she'd had. Her enthusiasm was catchy. We set a coffee-and-shoes date for the following Wednesday, and when she left, I found myself grinning. I hadn't made a new friend in so long, it felt like a treat.

'A girl died.'

Way to burst my bubble, Thibault. 'What are you talking about?'

He held his phone up to me. 'The incident Marie mentioned? I looked it up. Apparently, this girl was trying to show off, so she climbed onto the side of one of their inflatables and loosened the safety net. She fell and died in hospital.'

I grimaced. 'That's terrible. No wonder she looked guilty. It might not have been her fault, but it was her slide. She must have felt responsible in a way. Especially when people start pointing fingers.' Poor Marie.

'So you think it was an accident?'

'Why not? Maybe whoever sent the letters found out about this and played into her sense of guilt.'

'Unless they knew the whole thing had not been an accident, and now they're dead.'

I wrinkled my nose. 'Unlikely.'

'Is it? The whole thing fits, Julie. You just don't want to see it because you like her.'

I opened my mouth for a retort but closed it again, shocked. Was he right? But then, maybe I didn't want to assume his guilt because I liked him, too. I should bring up the sinister transfer between Tariel and him, but how?

'So, you hungry?'

I blinked at the rapid change of subject. 'Err, I suppose?' We could talk while cooking. But what if my instinct was wrong, my suspicions were right, and he really was here for the family? 'I don't really feel like cooking, though. Let's eat at Jeanette's.'

Though I avoided looking at his face, I could see the slight frown and the tightening of his lips. They passed quickly, but I felt that perhaps my mistrust wasn't entirely unjustified.

While we strolled to the village, I couldn't shake that uneasy feeling. There was something else, though, that wanted my attention, and I couldn't put my finger on what it was. At first I thought it was Marie's situation I felt sorry for, but that wasn't it. It was something she'd said, but the exact thing escaped my grasp every time I thought I had it. Shaking my head, I decided not to dwell on it. If it was important, it would come back to me. For now, I had an important conversation with my assistant to avoid.

19

You coming?

Jeanette's place was busy when we arrived. The restaurant was about the right size for a village of less than twelve hundred people, but Théo's food attracted outsiders as well. Good thing they'd got the permit to revive the old hotel. Pride of my first investment outside of my own business filled my heart. Yes, it was only money, but for my friend, it was a dream that I could help come true.

Plates stacked on her arms, Jeanette greeted us heartily when we walked in. All the outside tables had been taken, but Beau had spotted an empty space in the corner.

'Hello you! I'm thinking you're into *magret de canard* today, yes?'

I hadn't thought about what I was going to have, but now that she mentioned it... I nodded.

'Hi! I've seen you before, haven't I? Few nights ago? I'm Jeanette, Julie's friend. What can I get you?'

'*Salut*, Julie's friend. I'm her new assistant, Thibault.'
He flashed his swoon-worthy smile. 'I hear you do a good
andouillette.'

'The best.' She left us with a wink, which was her usual and
didn't mean anything special.

'Why didn't she take our drinks order?' Beau asked.

This confused me for a second. 'Oh. She knows what I like.
She always just brings you the wine that goes with the meal.'

'What if I didn't want to drink?'

See, this is why I never felt at home in the city. The possibility
of not drinking wine with *déjeuner* would never have crossed
my mind. 'Then you don't drink it. Drink your water instead.'
I demonstratively filled our glasses from the carafe.

Ordinarily, when I went to Jeanette's for lunch, I'd take a
book, so I'd be left in peace. Now Beau was here, I'd have no
other option than to talk with him.

'So, erm...'

'Hm?' He took out his phone and began scrolling.

How would I even start? Accuse him? 'I saw you! What
did Tariel give you?' Be obvious? 'So, how is Cyprien these
days?' Be direct? 'I know you're here to spy on me. Why?'
With the words forming in my mind, I realised how utterly
paranoid I would sound if my mother was right. Was I seeing
threats where there weren't any? I shivered with that vague

undercurrent of threat that had never left me in the past four years.

Thibault was right there. I could ask him. But he was already suspicious. He never took out his phone if there was a chance to talk to anyone. Perhaps I should wait for a little liquid courage.

Thibault had situated himself with his back to the café. It made sense for me to squish myself in the corner, since I took up less space, so I scanned the café. Familiar faces all around. The woman with the baby, she had been a year below me in school. The bald man used to feed the birds in the square on Saturday mornings. Did he still do that? Those two used to hate each other. Now they were staring into each other's eyes over forgotten pasta. And that man, he should have stopped two glasses of wine ago. Oh, crap, he'd spotted me.

'Madame Belmain!' Monsieur Durand slurred, just a tad too loudly. 'She left me.'

Oh dear. Wasn't there someone else he could go bother?

'Shtupid letterzh.'

The mother cooed to her child, the old man opened a newspaper. Staring contest still going strong. Beau no more than lifted an eyebrow, then went back to his phone. Ugh. I was stuck.

'She jusht went. Jusht like that.'

Why didn't Beau interfere? Oh, he was looking up pictures of some motorbike.

'How could she just leave?'

Yep, full-on wail had started.

'Shtupid letter.'

Going into repetition now. I zoned out, waiting for my food.

'It wazhn't true anyway, whazzit?'

Probably not. How had Laura put up with this man for so long? I'd have skipped town years ago. In fact, that's exactly what I had done. On the other hand, this must not be Monsieur Durand at his best. What did I know about them, anyway? Laura had made an effort to fit in. All the people I'd talked to knew her, but she'd still felt like an outsider. Would that happen to me? Even after befriending another outsider this morning, would I ever really be part of this community again?

Apolline had said she was Laura's friend. I straightened. In fact, she had spoken in past tense before correcting herself. Was that before or after I'd told her Laura was missing? I tried to replay our conversation in my head, but I couldn't remember. Then again, it didn't matter, did it? Laura was on her way to her mother. At least she had a mother to run to. Mine was here, just as I was. Had I run to my mother? It didn't feel like I did.

Beau sat up, but whatever he was looking at on his phone was more important than my predicament because he still hadn't caught on. Durand was wailing more loudly now. Something about him being mad, or her thinking he'd be mad? I was about to get mad myself! I'd come here to accuse my friend of betraying me, and instead I get a drunk neighbour hounding me. Where was the fairness in that?

When Jeanette brought our food, she brought Durand his bill, which I thanked her for with a grateful look. Beau also put his phone away, but when he looked around, he frowned.

'What's Cyprien doing here?'

My blood pressure spiked. 'What? Where?'

Beau inclined his head towards the bar. A short man with caramel-coloured hair had his back turned to me. I wouldn't have recognised him if Beau hadn't pointed him out. Before my marriage with Franck, I'd considered Cyprien my friend as well. But when Franck turned sour, it became painfully obvious where Cyprien's loyalties lay. Literally. When I first mentioned divorce, Cyprien had cornered me and twisted my arm behind me. 'You'd better think carefully about your next move,' he'd whispered. 'Because your life could become very difficult without Franck's protection.' He'd used a matter-of-fact tone, even smiling at me while he said it, but I'd never seen eyes that cold. My last drop of faith in Franck disappeared soon after, when I told him about our encounter, and all Franck did was shrug.

A shiver ran down my spine. One thing gave me a little bit of hope, though. If Thibault was surprised to see Cyprien here, then they wouldn't be in it together. Whatever 'it' was. If there was an 'it'. That last bit I heard in my mother's voice. But there had to be, right? There was absolutely nothing for Cyprien in a village like this. Except in this particular village, there was me. The chance that my mother was right, and his appearance here had nothing to do with me, was minimal.

The person at the bar laughed. He stood and left the café without showing me his face, but Thibault was right, it was definitely Cyprien. Though I'd lost all appetite, I managed to eat about half of what was on my plate. Once or twice I thought Thibault was glaring at me, but he looked away before I could catch him. Not talking to him felt more and more cowardly, but it was clear that he wasn't going to initiate anything either. We walked back to the house in uncharacteristic silence.

I let us both into the studio, still under a blanket of silence. When I saw Thibault hesitating in the middle of the room, I sighed.

'I give up.'

That earned me a puzzled look.

I perched on the white leather couch and threw a defeated hand in the air. 'This murder business? I thought I could help Jacqueline out, but I suppose detective business is none of my business. Everyone I've talked to lacks motive, opportunity, or the right knowledge about the means. For all I know, Cyprien did it! He's the only one I know who's capable of murder.'

Crossing his arms over his chest, Thibault huffed.

'Well, you tell me why he suddenly turns up in my village, looking for a house.'

Another puzzled look. 'Who says he's looking for a house?'

I swallowed. 'You know why I turned so pale at Tariel's?'

His expression turned wary. 'No?'

'I saw his name on an application form. He's going to live here.' I studied Beau's face and posture. If he was going to give any indication, I needed to pick up on it.

He knew what that name meant to me. He had been there when Franck uttered his threat, and he knew the connection between those men. But did his serious attitude mean bad news for me? All Thibault did was narrow his eyes. 'I did not know about that, Julie.'

'I take it he's not the changed man my mother hoped he'd be?' I felt my hands shake and balled my fists.

'No.' He paused, thinking as his eyebrows drew together. 'Is that why you've been so grumpy?'

'*I'm* grumpy?'

Letting out a deep breath, he dropped his arms to his sides. He studied me for a moment before taking the two strides that separated us and sitting down next to me, one knee on the couch so he was facing me. 'Juju, he and I are not on the same side. I told you I escaped, and that was the truth. It was better for everyone that I left.'

'I...' I cast down my eyes, remembering that I hadn't told him any of this before because I suspected him. It seemed ridiculous now. 'But why are you in cahoots with Tariel?'

'What?' He seemed genuinely confused.

'I saw you laughing together.'

'When?'

'The other night. He came here and he gave you something.'

Realisation dawned, but then his body shook with a barely held snort. 'His business card! He'd forgotten to give me his card after your little episode. Which, by the way, makes me think much less of your acting skills.'

I shot him some daggers. 'Thanks for taking the situation so seriously.'

His face sobered as he looked me in the eye. 'What do you want me to say? I don't think Cyprien has it in for you? I don't. Why he's decided to look for a house here... I can't answer that. But are you going to sit here and tremble just because you've seen him around? That's not the Julie I used to know!'

I gave him a doleful look. 'That was a long time ago.'

Frowning, he shook his head. 'Not for someone to change that much. I've seen you behind the camera, Juju. *That's* you. That's lively, funny, uninhibited you. The one that makes friends wherever she goes and could make a cardboard box feel like home. But you take one look at that rat, and you turn into a shivering, insecure mess? He may not have forgotten about you, but neither have I. You can't allow Franck or Cyprien or anyone else to take that spirit away from you. It's still in there.'

I was on the verge of tears. Had I really been like that? If I had, that spirit was long gone.

'You used to be one of my best friends, Julie. I came to you for a reason. Look at what you did.' He spread his arms and waved them around my studio. 'Franck left you with no money and a giant dent in your confidence. But despite that, you refused your family's money and you built your own business. You say your aunt gave you this house, but you bought it off her.'

'Mmm,' I interrupted but had to swallow before I could talk. 'That wasn't nearly what this place is worth.'

'Could you have bought it?'

'Well, yes. But—'

'Same thing. You made a lot of money, all on your own.'

'Not true. I had a lot of clients who followed me from my beauty blog.'

Beau sat back, his eyebrows raised in the most puppy-like expression. 'Don't you see? That's exactly it. You attract people. People like you, so they stick around and help you if you need it.' He flashed a lopsided grin. 'Even if you don't.'

I swallowed again, but it couldn't stop my tears from overflowing. I didn't think he was right, but it sure was sweet of him to say. He sighed and wrapped his arms around me, which didn't help at all with the waterworks. Still, I made a mental note: get more Beau-hugs.

When he leaned back, he frowned at his shoulder. 'Now look at me. You got mascara all over my shirt. Hang on, I'll go change.'

Getting up from the couch, he stripped his shirt off. That did help with the waterworks. My goodness, the boy was gorgeous. Where was my camera?

As it turned out, Thibault was a terrible model. For all his beauty, he just would not listen to me. It should have annoyed me, but after the pep talk of the decade, who could blame me for smiling and going with it? Even knowing Cyprien was probably still in the village didn't bother me so much now I knew I had Thibault on my side.

I'd thought up several poses that might be interesting: shirt caught in drawer, shirt caught on nail, shirt caught between lift doors. Yes, a lot of caught shirts. And I didn't even have a lift. But look at him! Why was he wearing shirts at all? The problem was that he was enjoying it all far too much. I could not get him to make a surprised face, or a slightly annoyed face, or any kind of face at all other than his happiest, broadest smile. Sure, it was a pretty smile, but it was hardly what I was going for.

'You know what? Lose the shirt altogether and drape yourself over the Harley. Let's see what we end up with there.'

I picked a book from the shelf at random. Maybe if I could get him to read, he'd forget to smile.

'Can you... sort of... lie down on it?'

He chuckled. 'And how am I supposed to do that?'

He straddled the bike, and— Ooh! Click.

I handed him the book. 'Just make yourself comfortable.'

'You want me to read *Little Women*?'

Oh. 'Can't go wrong with the classics. Bend over a little. Little more. Turn your right shoulder up. Put your hand on your knee. Now slide it up. Stop. Beautiful.'

'How am I supposed to read, when you keep interrupting?'

He looked up in mock irritation. Click. Finally!

'Yes! Okay, now turn around.' He turned his torso and I clicked. 'I meant sit backwards on the bike.'

'No.'

'Why not?'

'Because of the shape of the saddle. Stop being so controlling! I thought this was supposed to be fun.'

'It is for my clients. You're only—'

Controlling? I lowered my camera, thoughts and memories passing at full speed. 'Beau... We never considered—'

A frantic knock on the wooden courtyard door cut me off.

When I opened the door, Lucas stormed into the courtyard. Hair dishevelled and breath heavy, he didn't even seem to notice Thibault. His eyes locked onto mine and did not let go.

'Where's Tiana?'

I recoiled from the intensity in his voice and from the corner of my eye I saw Beau dismount. 'I don't know.'

What had happened? Did Lucas turn out to be a mental case after all, sending Tiana into hiding? From the wild look in his eyes, I could almost believe it. But at second glance, it looked more like worry than madness.

'Look, she's perfectly capable of taking care of herself. She grew up here. Wherever she is, chances are she's not in any kind of trouble.'

Lucas raked a hand through his hair, looking between Beau and me. 'I wanted to show her this.' He waved a piece of thick, cream-coloured paper with a few handwritten lines on it. 'But she's not answering any of my calls or texts, and she's not at home. I don't know where else to look.'

Thibault joined us, tugging his shirt back on. 'What is that?'

'It's...' Lucas hesitated, clutching the letter closer to his chest. Then he sighed. 'It's my letter.'

'But it's—'

'Different, I know.' Staring at the letter in his hand, he continued, 'I realised that as soon as you mentioned yours. Maybe I should have spoken up then, but...'

'Yours is real.' I placed my hand on his arm. 'You don't have to tell us what's in it.'

Beau's face lit up. 'That means I was right!'

'It would appear so, yes,' I admitted.

The victory lap seemed a little inappropriate given Lucas's state, but Lucas only raised his eyebrows.

'That the letters were sent by two different people, and we'd only seen the ones nobody cared about,' I explained. 'The ones sent to confuse people as to who had got a real one. But since you're the first person we've seen with an original letter that preventative measure did the opposite of what it was supposed to. It only served to highlight the fact that poison pen letters were involved.' I bit my bottom lip. 'Can you tell us who it's from?'

Again, Lucas stared at the letter. 'It doesn't say. I racked my brain for ages to find out who could have known about this, but the only person I can come up with is the murdered lady, Madame Braymand.'

Thibault went off on another victory lap, while I nodded. 'That makes sense.'

'Not to me. At least not at first. I...' A muscle in his jaw flexed. 'I used to be married. I'm not ashamed of that, but my ex wouldn't leave me alone. I more or less fled the States and hid here. This letter threatens to tell my ex where to find me. There are so few people that know both my situation and my location that I couldn't work out who would send me such a threat. But then I remembered the last official letters regarding the matter went out right after I settled here. If someone had managed to get a look at them... I still hadn't figured out who it could have been, until Tiana told me about the disgruntled ex-postal employee. No evidence, though, mind you.'

'And Ti doesn't answer your calls because...?' I know, it was pure curiosity. But I reckon Lucas gave me permission to be nosy by storming into my courtyard telling me his other secrets. Why not share this as well? He did give me a bit of a side-eye, but then probably came to the same conclusion.

'I... avoided contact with her yesterday.'

It was all I could do not to roll my eyes.

'She told me how she was looking for True Love Forever, and here I was hiding from my ex-wife, who'd pulled another dumb stunt that I had to call her about yesterday. I just needed some time to... you know...'

'Hm,' I said to my phone screen, tapping out a text to Tiana. When I looked up, the two men were doing some sort of male, coded, eye communication thing. It made no sense to me, but it seemed to calm Lucas down, so, with a mental shrug, I moved on. 'I think—'

And then my phone rang.

'That'll be her now.'

It wasn't. It was Jacqueline.

'Hi, Jacquie, I was just about to call you. I think I know what happened.'

Jacqueline's voice was flat and uninterested. That's when I remembered our tiff. 'Tell me in half an hour. We'll be paying a visit to Durand, so if it's important, I'll drop by.'

Somehow I felt deflated. I'd thought I'd have news for her. 'Oh, so you already knew?'

In the brief silence that followed, my phone vibrated.

'Hang on, let me check this text.'

I tapped the notification to get through to Tiana's text.

On my way to see you. Just dropping something at Durand's.

I frowned, making Lucas jump back into antsy mode. Putting the phone on speaker, I asked, 'Jacqueline... What did you call me about?'

'Oh, you know, your neighbour? She never arrived at her mother's. Thought you'd like to—'

'You'd better come over. Like, right now!'

The rise in my voice had alerted Lucas. He was at the door before I'd ended the call.

But Beau wasn't so quick. His confused gaze flicked from Lucas to me. 'What are we doing?'

'Making sure Durand doesn't kill Tiana. You coming?'

20

Just some autumn cleaning

The late afternoon sun caressed Tiana's face as she strolled down the hill, shoe box tucked under her arm. Life was pretty good. She'd written almost four thousand words today, meaning she could still write just fine without the attentions of a handsome gardener. If he turned out to have a legitimate reason for the radio silence yesterday, and that's why he'd left about a hundred messages while she was writing, she might consider adding him to her already pretty good life. As long as he kept it that way.

She had to admit, though, taking her phone off silent mode after her writing sprint and finding all those messages? Felt pretty good. She smiled up at the sun. Yes, pretty good.

She hadn't answered any of them, though. She hadn't even opened them. What if the news was bad? Not that he'd leave that many messages just to say he wasn't interested. Right? But still, she wanted to bask in the possibilities a little longer. Maybe show Julie her phone, with the number of messages prominently displayed. Not a bad idea! She could drop off those silly boots while she was at it.

So here she was, sun on her face, boots almost gone, and such a lot of words done! People in this village might not be talking about her, but that didn't mean she wasn't interesting. She had loads of fans, and not a day went by that she didn't have a sweet email in her inbox declaring how much her words meant to that reader. She mattered. Why she'd let some man make her doubt herself was inexplicable. It was also temporary. She'd pulled herself together, switched off her phone, wrote like a madwoman, and had emerged on the other side of her sprint with all those messages.

Well, all right. If he was that willing, then she might be persuaded to admit him once more into her life. She smiled again as she stepped up to Laura Durand's front door and knocked. Laura hadn't answered her message either. But she'd had two months to come up with a reasonable explanation for the addition of a pair of expensive boots, and if they stayed at Tiana's, they wouldn't do her any good either.

The door opened, and Monsieur Durand's flustered head appeared around it. *'Oui?'*

She held up the box. 'These are Laura's. I've had them for a while, so now I'm returning them.' It was a bit of a flaky explanation, but she'd leave that to Laura.

'Oh. Erm...' Monsieur Durand held out a hand, but it was already clutching a stained cloth, so he had to open the door wider in order to hold out his other hand. His rumpled clothes were wet in places, showing smudges of the same reddish-brown stain that covered the cloth. When he noticed Tiana staring, he let out a nervous chuckle. 'Jusht some shpring... I mean autumn cleaning.'

Still holding out the box to him, Tiana gave a half smile. Was he drunk? Her phone pinged, and when Durand finally took the box, she answered Julie's text.

'Who's that? What are you telling them?'

Raising her eyebrows, Tiana looked up. It was an oddly nosey question to begin with, but especially so for someone like Monsieur Durand. She saw him realise it, then panic, drop the box, and grab her wrist. With a surprisingly strong tug, he pulled her inside, her phone crashing on the gravel of the driveway.

'What—'

He slammed the door shut, dragging her into the living room.

Tiana pulled on her arm, but Durand held fast, panic now obvious in his eyes. Droplets of sweat appeared on his brow, and his breath came in short bursts.

'Let go of me! Why—'

'Hush! Who did you tell about the blood?'

'What blood?' What was he talking about?

Durand pointed at the coffee table with his free hand. 'The bl— Oh. Oh no.' Like a leaf in the wind, his panic turned to anger. 'Why did you text? Now what am I going to do with you?'

Though Tiana had been too surprised to feel anything else up till now, a rising dread crept up her spine. Do with her? Blood? What had he been doing when she interrupted him? Without taking her eyes off him for too long, Tiana glanced around the room. Other than a bucket of soapy water, she didn't see anything suspicious. If he hadn't mentioned blood, not even the bucket would have seemed out of place.

Out of nowhere, Durand's fist landed in Tiana's stomach, and she doubled over, gasping for breath. He took off his belt, and pulled her hands together behind her back, pushing her face down on the couch.

All the while, he kept mumbling, 'It was an accident. Who's going to believe that now? Women. Always meddling. Can't trust them to do anything right.'

Tiana took in a few large gulps of air, but by the time she could think about anything other than breathing, her hands were tied. She tried to push to her knees, but Durand planted his foot on her back and put the soapy rag in her mouth.

'You will not—'

A bang on the front door, followed by shouting in at least two voices, made Durand freeze.

'Who...?'

Glass shattered in a front room. Durand didn't seem to think twice. He ran out the garden door not two seconds before Lucas stormed into the room. The thunder on his face transformed into worry when he noticed Tiana. Kneeling beside her, he took the gag out of her mouth and started on the knot in the belt.

'Are you okay?'

All she could do was nod. Why was Lucas here? How did he know? She was ready to believe he was a superhero when Thibault came in, followed by Julie. Beau sprinted after Durand, but Julie, face lined with apprehension, stumbled towards the couch. She grabbed Tiana's hand as soon as it came loose, and stroked her hair.

'Thank goodness you're okay. We came as soon as you texted. Did he hurt you?'

Tiana eased Julie's hand off her head as she sat up. 'I'm fine. Don't worry.' Blushing, she turned to Lucas. 'Thank you.'

Beau came back in, dragging a struggling Durand along, who cursed him for all he could think of. Tiana flinched, inadvertently rubbing her stomach.

Lucas frowned as he rose. 'What did he do?'

But before Tiana could answer, he'd turned and closed the distance to Durand. Thibault took one look at Lucas and released the little man, who had about half a second of surprise left before Lucas raised his fist and punched him in the jaw. Monsieur Durand whimpered, protesting the unfairness of two against one, but it was lost in the sound of banging on the front door. Through the broken window, Jacqueline's voice sounded ominous.

'Police! Open this door.'

21

Nobody cares about your divorce!

I hurried to obey Jacqueline's demand. While Durand deserved that punch, I didn't know Lucas well enough to know if he'd stop.

As soon as I opened the door, Jacqueline barged in, followed by Marc Froment, who looked like he was out for blood.

Assessing the situation in the living room, the first thing Jacqueline asked was, 'Monsieur Durand, are you all right?'

Durand was holding his jaw, but after a glance at Lucas, seemed to think it wiser to nod than to complain. No one else said a word, all of us staring either at the floor or at Durand or Jacqueline, who was a little scary when she went all policewoman.

'Is anyone going to tell me what happened?'

I scraped my throat. 'I thought you knew?'

'What am I supposed to know?'

'That he killed his wife.' I pointed at Durand.

Jacqueline raised her eyebrows at me, then trained her piercing stare on Durand, who whimpered again.

'I didn't! She fell. Well, I pushed her... But she went to her mother's.'

'Madame Durand's mother called us. Your wife never arrived at her destination.'

'Of course not, she's dead.' Jacqueline's glare told me to shut up, but I knew I was right. 'Go check Auguste's *cuves*.'

Now everybody stared at me. I explained that I'd seen bloody scratches on Durand's hands and blackberry stains on his trousers the day before, and the abandoned *cuves* in the field between our houses were covered in brambles. They'd be the perfect hiding place for a body. Jacqueline narrowed her eyes, clearly doubting my reasoning, but Durand's eyes bulged. He opened and closed his mouth like a fish, then sank down on a chair.

'Where are these tanks?' Jacqueline now asked. When I told her, she sent Marc Froment out to check them, while she took a notebook out of her pocket. 'Monsieur Durand?'

He clapped his hands over his mouth, rubbing the sides of his nose. 'It was an accident.' From the corner of my eye, I saw Tiana nod. Durand sighed, a deep, sorrowful sigh. 'When I came into the room, Laura was going through a notebook. I wouldn't even have noticed, except she looked so guilty and tried to hide it from me.

'All I did was ask what she had, and she burst into tears. She said it was Claire Braymand's notebook, where she kept all her secrets. Laura had taken it away so nobody would suspect what she had done.' A sob escaped before he could continue. 'Still I didn't realise what she meant. She started accusing me, saying it was my fault. I should have trusted her more and given her more. That she wouldn't have had to keep things secret then, and none of "this" would have happened.

'Suddenly, she stopped crying and smiled. Said she'd been smart about it, sending all those letters out beforehand. With this book, she could send more and nobody would ever know.' Durand let his gaze wander around the room. 'That's when I started to make sense of her story. She must have had a secret. Something she'd never told me. Something Madame Braymand had uncovered and somehow held over her head. But even with that terrible suspicion growing, in my fear I still couldn't believe she'd do what she seemed to have done. Not my Laura. So meek and loving? She wouldn't... kill someone?'

He pressed his palms to his eyes and took a faltering breath. 'But she had. I couldn't believe it. I stared at her, and she laughed. She waved the notebook in my face and told me people would pay to keep these secrets hidden. Braymand had been a fool not to exploit her knowledge, other than to show her power over people. Laura said she could make us good money, and she wouldn't have to ask me for anything ever again.'

Tears streaming over his cheeks, he looked up at Jacqueline. 'She was right. It was my fault. I knew she wanted more. She deserved more. I should have given her more. Then maybe she wouldn't have—' He sobbed again. 'My fault.' Another sob. 'When I realised that, I... I pushed her away. She tripped. Fell... her head...' Staring at the corner of the low table, he reached up and touched the side of his head.

Then he sighed again, wiping his cheeks dry. 'I hid her. I'm sorry. I didn't know what else to do.' He looked at Tiana. 'When you knocked, I'd just found blood underneath the table that I was trying to clean up. I panicked. I'm deeply sorry for hitting you.'

Jacqueline stepped forward. 'Pierre Durand, I'm arresting you for...'

Pierre! I didn't even hear the rest. His name was Pierre. I didn't think I'd ever heard it before, not even when he introduced himself. Not that it mattered now. I'd probably have new neighbours to introduce myself to soon. Why had I not made more effort to get to know my own neighbours in the past three months? I'd had no idea what took place right next door. If I had, could I have prevented what had happened? I could have talked to Laura. I knew a thing or two about being controlled... Whether it's about money or about who you can and can't see, lack of control can lead you to do crazy things sometimes.

One being driven to murder, and one guilty of doing the driving.

As Jacqueline led him away, I took a step to follow her, but then noticed the empty couch. I stopped and turned, looking around the room, but both Tiana and Lucas had disappeared. The only person left was Beau, grinning at me like a fool. He jerked his head towards the open garden door. Sure enough, Lucas and Tiana were outside. Lip-locked.

I invited Beau in since I couldn't very well send him away without dinner. Before I'd shut the door behind us, however, I saw Céline walk up to the studio door.

'He's in here, Céline,' I called out. 'Come on in.'

Thibault was already in the kitchen, filling the kettle. My thoughts exactly, I could use a *tisane*. Some herbal tea might settle my nerves. It didn't seem like something Beau would crave though. And that suspicion was confirmed when he took a beer from the fridge. He'd filled the kettle for me. Dang it, his charm offensive was working.

Céline swatted at Beau's arm, waving her phone. 'All caps and five exclamation marks. I knew it was urgent, but then I had to figure out what "cpmr ti dufpue" meant. Switch on predictive text, will you? By the time I'd deciphered your code, there wasn't anyone there. What was so important?'

Thibault related the whole story from the moment Lucas came in, not forgetting the arm waves, the superlatives, and, of course, embellishing his own role in the matter. Apparently, little Durand had fought like a lion before Beau managed to restrain him. Unfortunately for Beau, Céline saw right through all that and simply turned to me.

'How awful! I still can't believe she would do such a thing. She always seemed so sweet.' She touched her hand to her throat and swallowed.

'People can be terrible when cornered.' I knew that all too well. And I would feel the guilt of not talking to Laura sooner for a long time.

'So how did you figure out it must have been the Durands?'

Sipping from my *tisane*, I nodded towards Thibault. 'He called me overbearing.'

He fished a little sketchbook out of his back pocket and started to doodle. 'I said controlling. You are.'

The word stung. More than I wanted it to. More than I would ever allow anyone to see. I waved a dismissive hand. 'My first reaction to that was to tell him he was obstinate, and maybe he should be more submissive.' Where had I heard those words before? I almost shuddered. 'But then it reminded me of the relationship between the Durands, and how I might have reacted to being ruled by my husband.' How I did react.

I took a deep breath, banishing the memories. 'Tiana's story about a woman hiding boots from her husband suddenly fell into place. She must have been talking about them. So Madame Durand almost certainly kept secrets from her husband. It wasn't such a big leap to assume she'd had a letter about it. A real one, different from all the silly ones everyone was talking about. Lucas confirmed the existence of two separate sets of letters when he showed me his. That one was of a quality befitting a sender who had owed her position in the village to people posting letters. She made sure people paid attention to letters again – paid attention to *her*. But to someone harbouring a secret, the threat of being exposed makes a great motive.' I counted motive off on my fingers.

'Means took me longer to figure out. From what Apolline had said, I believed she took Laura Durand under her wing when foraging. However, Marie Madora told me Apolline had... exaggerated her role. That meant it was Laura Durand who had the botanical knowledge Apolline Bailly tried to claim. That's means' – I raised another finger – 'she certainly had plenty of opportunity. I looked up colchicum, what Lucas called naked ladies, and it's a little purple flower that blooms in autumn. Like a crocus, but without any leaves. Now that I knew what to look for, I've seen them all over the village, but also in Laura Durand's garden. In fact, she was the only person regularly visiting Claire Braymand. What if it was less caring, and more pleading mercy? Laura herself had told me she was glad to be rid of Madame Braymand. She even asked me if I thought she was a bad person.'

I bit my lip. I'd told her nobody would think of her as bad. How was I to know how much that would change?

'Of course, it was just a theory, and one that only flashed through my mind when Thibault called me controlling, but it did fit. Her sudden disappearance, however, didn't fit anywhere. Also, why would Durand have looked for his wife amid the brambles? I recognised the stains when I saw them, but he'd covered up the scratches on his hands by playing with a red pen. I'd noticed them, but with everything else that was going on, I let myself be fooled that they weren't important. The man was looking for his distraught wife, why not look in illogical places?

'Then when Laura didn't show up at her mother's, things finally clicked. It was an act. Durand had said it himself in the café – his wife had thought he'd be angry. When he found out what she'd done, he was. Suddenly, the stains and the timing made sense. The fact that he'd tried to cover up the scratches only incriminated him.'

Céline had listened open-mouthed. 'But how did you know Tiana was in danger?'

I huffed out a laugh. 'I didn't. Ordinarily, I would never have even considered the possibility, but Lucas had me jittery, and Jacqueline called at the exact right moment. Even going over there, I considered that we were overreacting, but then we saw the discarded shoe box outside. I thought Lucas would explode. Also, Beau...' I turned, waiting for him to look up from his drawing. 'If we ever have to break in through a window again, just go in ahead of me and open the door. No need to show off when we're on a rescue mission.' Of course, it was difficult not to like being picked up like I weighed nothing.

Thibault glanced at Céline, but she grinned at me. She probably saw through me as well.

I smiled back, then downed the rest of my *tisane*. 'There's only one thing I'm still not sure on. Marie Madora knew Laurent Tariel visited Claire Braymand. But Braymand's house is well out of the way, so she couldn't have noticed it in passing. She did say she wanted to visit, though. Maybe the reason she couldn't after all was that she saw Tariel there. I can always ask her next Wednesday.'

'Are you sure you want to bring that up?' Beau asked, barely looking up from his sketchbook.

Huh. I hadn't expected him to comment on my social behaviour, but he might be right. Perhaps reminding my new friend of a sad thing in her past was not the most friendly thing to do. It had been too long since I'd had to behave like a friend. Tiana didn't count. She already knew me too well. But anyone else in this village?

'Well done, though,' Céline said. Her face was serious. 'Who knows what would have happened if you hadn't shown up.'

I stared at the cat flap where, on cue, Henri came in and jumped on my lap. 'I should have shown up much earlier. Maybe I could have helped.'

Beau frowned at his drawing, but Céline only shrugged. 'Who says she would have opened up to you? You can't help everyone, much as you may try. But you certainly helped Tiana. You'll be the talk of the village by tonight.'

I sighed, not feeling much better. 'In that case, maybe they'll look past my failed marriage and my return with my tail between my legs.'

Now even Céline frowned. 'That's not how they see you.' She glanced at Beau, then back at me. 'Really, that's what you think?'

I cuddled Henri, regretting that I'd let slip my anxiety on the matter.

'Nobody cares about your divorce!' Her wide eyes showed nothing but sincerity.

It was sweet of her to say, but she was not the rest of the village.

'Franck was a bum, everybody knows that. They're proud to have a famous businesswoman among them.'

Henri purred in agreement.

A match lit a tiny flame inside me. 'I'm not famous.'

'You have an international clientèle. In this village, that means you're famous.'

Beau, back to drawing, nodded lazily.

The little flame grew. Maybe I didn't have to do this all alone. La Mademoiselle had been alone. She wasn't needed any more, but she still needed others. Yet instead of asking for help, she drove them all away. If I'd learnt anything, it was that I would not end up like that. Thibault had already said he would help, even if I didn't need it. In that case, the rest of the village could be my challenge. By this time next year, I could have lots of friends again. I beamed at Céline.

As one good turn deserves another, I studied Thibault. His knee rested against the kitchen table, making an upright surface for his sketchbook. We hadn't finished our shoot yet. Maybe having him here wasn't so bad after all. I'd kick him out tomorrow. Or maybe draw up a contract.

Other books by Christa Bakker

Sign up for a FREE Christmas story at

https://christabakker.com/newsletter

Acknowledgements

Kristen Tate of The Blue Garret did a marvelous job with the editing and dealing with my stubbornness. But, you know, when she's right, she's right!

Thank you to both my mother and my friend Carole Marples, who made sure my cast stayed manageable.

Nienke Grasset, you are a fount of French knowledge, and I am so grateful for your help!

Last but not least, thank you to my husband and children for not only putting up with me, but supporting me with not too many sighs and groans.

Though the author may have borrowed names and places from friends in France, none of the characters are based on actual people. The story, all names, characters, and incidents portrayed in this production are fictitious. No identification with actual persons (living or deceased), places, buildings, and products is intended or should be inferred.

Editing by Kristen Tate at The Blue Garret

Book cover by Christa and Erik Bakker

1st edition 2023

ISBN: 978-1-8383181-3-0

Visit the author's website at: www.christabakker.com